PETE RANDALL

a FUNNY old GAME

A timeless soccer match, between
friends who never grow old...

PETE RANDALL

a FUNNY old GAME

A timeless soccer match, between
friends who never grow old...

MEREO
Cirencester

Mereo Books

1A The Wool Market Dyer Street Cirencester Gloucestershire GL7 2PR
An imprint of Memoirs Publishing www.mereobooks.com

A Funny Old Game: 978-1-86151-439-4

First published in Great Britain in 2015
by Mereo Books, an imprint of Memoirs Publishing

The address for Memoirs Publishing Group Limited can be found at
www.memoirspublishing.com

The Memoirs Publishing Group Ltd Reg. No. 7834348

The Memoirs Publishing Group supports both The Forest Stewardship Council® (FSC®) and
the PEFC® leading international forest-certification organisations. Our books carrying both the
FSC label and the PEFC® and are printed on FSC®-certified paper. FSC® is the only
forest-certification scheme supported by the leading environmental organisations including
Greenpeace. Our paper procurement policy can be found at
www.memoirspublishing.com/environment

Typeset in 12/18pt Bembo
by Wiltshire Associates Publisher Services Ltd. Printed and bound in Great Britain by
Printondemand-Worldwide, Peteborough PE2 6XD

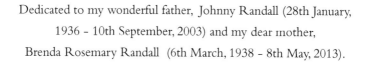

Dedicated to my wonderful father, Johnny Randall (28th January, 1936 – 10th September, 2003) and my dear mother, Brenda Rosemary Randall (6th March, 1938 – 8th May, 2013).

Always on my mind, and forever in my heart.

Chapter 1

Royston Lane had finished dropping in the preset for the matinee show and was routinely checking the brail-lines along the flyrail, 35 feet above the stage. He settled in the big, threadbare armchair at the end of the flyfloor and remembered that he'd been given something by a little girl as he'd been about to walk into the stage door. Leaning to his left, he picked up the rectangular package and sat it in his lap. Peering through his spectacles as he unwrapped the plain white plastic carrier bag, he held his breath as the timeworn, faded green book came into view.

It was a thick, heavy volume with no lettering on its binding or elsewhere on the cover. Discarding the carrier bag, Royston carefully opened the book and read the title page. The musty smell sprang from the thick white sheets like the dust of a fabulous elixir or the promise of adventure. He was already captivated. It read:

MYTH, MAGIC and LEGEND
by L. d'Altabar

The glare reflected up from the stage was dimmed as the working lights made way for the preset. The aged Anglepoise already at his shoulder, he scanned the first few pages, searching in vain for a date and failing also to find the printer's or publisher's mark. Strange, he thought to himself, already itching to read the introduction.

He cast his mind back to the little girl who had nonchalantly handed him the carrier bag only half an hour previously. There was something unsettling about her eyes, he remembered, causing him to avert his gaze while he formulated some sort of word of thanks, by which time she had vanished into the crowded street. Being slightly behind schedule, he had dashed straight up to the flyfloor. Only now did he begin to realize the seemingly random nature of the event. Why would a little girl give him this book and then just walk off without a word?

But something was drawing him back to the book. He had it open on the brief introduction but couldn't bring himself to start reading it yet. He knew that he'd become too engrossed in the thing and didn't want to miss any of the show's many flying cues. Taking one last sniff of the book's mysterious odour, he replaced it in the bag and prepared himself for another three hours of hauling ropes up in his lofty gantry, supplying everything from blue skies to castle walls for the show down below. Putting on his headset, he got up from the chair and grabbed hold of a rope that disappeared into the gloom above him, speaking softly into the headset microphone.

"Yeah, flys standing by cue one."

Easing off the handle of the brake and looking up at where a red light glowed on a small box on the end wall, he sniffed the air; it was rather like the smell from the book. The Nottingham Playhouse was hundreds of years old, built at the beginning of the twenty-first century and before mechanization was able to interfere with its overcomplicated hydraulics and advanced electronics. The flying tower was equipped with a centuries-old single-purchase counterweight system, lovingly maintained and entirely independent of computers. Despite being on a low wage, Royston and his fellow stagehands were fiercely proud to be working in one of the last surviving traditional theatres in the country.

The small band in the orchestra pit was nearing the end of the overture. Royston tensed, keeping his eyes fixed on the cue-light. Pulling down on the weight cradle when the green light came on, Royston whizzed the house tabs out super-fast, holding on to the ascending rope and using his weight to prevent the flying bar from crashing into the underside of the grid. Dropping lightly back to the floor, he put the brake on and tried to concentrate on how long it was till his next cue, while listening to the girl in the prompt corner telling everyone about the lovely restaurant her boyfriend had taken her to the previous night.

He looked down the long row of ropes and the cracked linoleum floor, imagining ghosts of previous flymen leaning on the flyrail and watching over everyone from the shadows upstage. Subconsciously he was certain they still lingered in the dusty recesses of the theatre, an entire backstage crew of guardian angels, no longer on the payroll but never missing a performance. Consciously, he would solemnly testify to anyone the same, though he would never be the one to broach the subject in the first place. For Royston Lane, it was all just part and parcel of the wonderful world of the stage; an invisible system of spiritual cogs within the physical wheels.

After curtain-down on the matinee show, he sat back in the chair, opened the mysterious book and read the introduction.

There are many who dismiss magic as nothing more than so much 'hocus-pocus'; there are those who explain away myth and legend as 'stuff and nonsense'. Thankfully, the large collection of ancient papers, scrolls and documents that verify the contents of this volume have been safely stored in Pudding Lane, London, so those who still choose to scoff can see for themselves the authenticity of the chapters contained herein. MYTH, MAGIC and LEGEND is the culmination of a lifetime's study of these divers and astonishing documents, presented, with full-colour illustrations, for children of all ages.

Somewhat puzzled by the text, Royston turned to the outline of a full-page picture on the other side. Carefully turning the page, he revealed a scene from an ancient city. There were men and women smiling and living in comfort and peace, fruit trees, children chasing after a ball. He read the title of the first chapter and shook his head in disbelief.

"Atlantis? No!" he muttered. Flicking back to the introduction, he wondered at that reference to Pudding Lane. Wasn't that where the Great Fire of London had started in the mid-17th century? And if it was, and the fire hadn't started yet, then when had this been written? Who was this L. d'Altabar anyway? Did the last scraps of evidence that these legends existed actually perish in the conflagration of 1666?

Surrendering to his curiosity, he went briefly through the book from front to back, only pausing to admire the faded colours of the illustrations and their scenes of heroism and derring-do. He decided to read it right through when he got home after the evening show. He spent the rest of his break eating his sandwiches and perusing the pictures, amazed at the atmosphere and sense of drama they conveyed.

The following morning, Royston's eight-year-old son, Mark, found the book on his bedside table. Thumbing through and becoming entranced by the book almost made him late for the school bus, and he made it with only seconds to spare. He spent the rest of the day with his imagination in overdrive, counting away the hours to the time when he would return home and devour the book greedily from beginning to end. This was unusual for the boy, as he normally reserved such excitement for football and had never, until now, had any feelings at all about books – even football books. But this was like no other volume he had ever seen before. It had elicited a thrill of wonder from him the moment he first saw it.

Mark completed his homework as soon as he returned from school. Having sat down for his evening meal with his brother, sister, father and mother, he swallowed the last mouthful of stew and asked to leave the table. Royston gave his permission and stood up himself.

"I'd best be off to work or I'll be late" he said. "Where

are you rushing off to, Mark? You're not actually going to *read* that book I left out for you, are you?"

The boy paused at the foot of the stairs and grinned back at his father.

"Yes, Dad! Can I? I've already done all my homework."

Mary verified this with a nod to her husband. Seven-year-old Will and ten-year-old Sarah exchanged baffled looks as they continued eating their meal.

"Of course you can, son," said Royston.

Twenty seconds later the boy was already wondering where Pudding Lane in London might be. His brother and sister were playing a football game on the large screen in the lounge downstairs; his father had gone out in the rain to work another show at the theatre, while his mother washed up the dinner dishes.

The rain pounded against the window of Mark's room as the book took him from Atlantis to Babylon via Lyonesse. His eyes shone as he drank in the wonderfully dated pictures, and his mind began to fill with visions of King Arthur, Robin Hood and heroes from thousands of years before.

He was halfway through the chapter on magic when his mother appeared at the door. "Hot milk and biscuits, Mark?"

He looked up at her for a fraction of a second before re-immersing himself in the book. "Yes please, Mum."

Mary walked over and looked at the picture of the boy

in the temple foundations, framed by bolts and flashes of lightning.

"Don't be up all night reading this, sweetheart. If you don't get your sleep…"

"I know. If I don't get my sleep I'll be tired in school and I won't learn anything."

She ruffled his hair and left the room, smiling.

Magic, said the book, was mostly being in possession of some knowledge that no one else was aware of, and using it to your advantage. When it went into all the various ways of foretelling the future, Mark's eight-year-old brain, despite its thirst for knowledge, began to boggle. He skipped the rest of that particular section and managed to read about a strange thing that had happened in the First World War, back in the early part of the twentieth century. He would read the whole of the magic chapter again when he was a little older, he decided.

The biscuits and milk consumed, Mark fought to keep his eyelids from closing. He breathed in the smell and tried to focus on the huge number of soldiers running to safety behind the line of ghostly archers in the picture. His dreams would never be the same again.

Chapter 2

MONDAY 28TH AUGUST, 1935 AD

Vague and distant traffic sounds came and went across the periphery of his hearing as the boy slipped into the chill whiteness of the scullery. Sleepy fingers fiddled with the back door latch, his full bladder urging haste, but resulting in less speed.

A minute later and he emerged from the outside privy, his bare feet feeling the cool flagstones of the yard as he returned to the kitchen sink for a wash. His head cleared while he leaned over the home-made tin bowl, taking deep draughts of ozone from the water which ran from the gnarled old faucet above the huge sink which, were it not for the even bigger Aga stove nearby, would have dominated the whole room.

For a moment, the boy left his hands in the water and listened to the distant drone of an aeroplane as it seemed to crawl slowly across the sky. Ten years old. Today.

Ten years old!

Today!

He closed his eyes and listened to the sound of his mother's footsteps coming down the stairs, savouring the moment and etching as much detail as possible into his memory, wanting this special time to last forever. The smell of a lifetime of toast mixed jarringly with odours from various soaps. He could still detect a whiff of the sprouts they had had with yesterday's Sunday roast.

"Hungry, love?"

He snapped his eyes open and aimed the brightest smile that he was able to muster at his mother. She beamed back at him blearily, ruffling his hair and moving with her usual effortless grace towards the kettle on the hob. His six-month-old sister was riding her mother's hip as she glided from the oven to the sink, watching everything with varying degrees of interest and picking her nose with nonchalance.

"I could probably eat a whole horse, being as how I'm *ten*!" he announced gleefully, the cold water splashing over his face and neck as he finished his ablutions. His mother placed the kettle on the hotplate and hugged him.

"Ugh!" he said, the soap in his eyes reducing his vision to a riot of exploding colours.

"Ugh!" he said again as his mother, still bearing baby Janet, hugged her son, while the little one managed to yank at a handful of his hair and dribble down the back of his neck.

"Happy birthday, Paul! What's it like being a grown man then, eh, my little soldier?"

Paul forced the towel deep into his eye sockets to clear away the stinging soap. Then he tried to reach his sister's spittle with it before it trickled all the way down to the back of his clean underpants - unsuccessfully. He sat at the small wooden dining table and looked thoughtful before answering. His mother was working her magic with the bread and the teapot.

He found himself staring at the wooden radio that had always been there on the shelf next to the family portrait taken on the beach at Weston, and the sepia photograph of his grandfather from 1890. But it was the radio that had his attention now. He tried to imagine the tangle of wires and valves that lurked beneath its smooth, modern exterior. It always worried him somehow that he had not an inkling of how it worked; he equated the whole beastly mess to one of the seemingly impossible tasks which, he assumed, grown-ups had to tackle as one of the many trials of adulthood.

"We-ell," he began, frowning at the smug teak finish of the radio, "am I old enough to be a professional football player yet?"

His mother put a piece of buttered toast and a scalding cup of tea in front of him.

"Thanks, mum." Abstractedly, he munched on the toast as he watched his little sister try to eat some of the hair that she had just liberated from her brother's scalp.

"We've talked about this, Paul" she hissed quietly, though there was no one to overhear. "Yer father says he won't have any son of his playing kiddies' games all his life. You'll have to get a proper job when the time comes and hope they let you have Saturdays off – if you *must* play these games!" She was trying to sound astonished that he was still harbouring ideas of being a footballer, though they both knew that she secretly approved of his dream.

Paul rolled his eyes and moved his eyebrows up and down. "Yes, *mother!*" His father might lack interest in sport, but he could have clipped boys around the ear for England at an international level.

He put the half-eaten piece of toast back onto the plate and reached for his tea, just as little Janet sneezed. Bringing the cup to his mouth, he narrowed his eyes and just avoided getting a mouthful of something that had some of his hair in it.

"Ugh!" he said. He put the cup back down, untasted, and noticed that his darling baby sister had also managed to project something similar over his toast. Completely unfazed and totally at one with everything, his mother replaced his tea and toast in a trice and was now ironing from a huge pile of washing in a basket on the easy chair in the far corner.

Janet was now busy wiping something that looked quite like porridge over her face as she sat in her rickety wooden highchair across the table from Paul, singing a lilting nonsense song about nothing in particular.

Paul's mother watched him as he, in turn, carefully watched his sister's every move. Janet looked at him, giggled happily, and spewed out a stream of porridge back into her bowl. Quietly, his mother got up and went out to the cupboard under the stairs in the passageway as Paul continued to flinch at his sister's every burp and belch. His mother came back in and put a large brown paper bag on the table in front of him. She leaned over and kissed his forehead.

"Happy birthday, sweetheart!" she said, returning to her ironing and her own cup of tea. Paul's eyes widened and his mouth formed an 'O'. A ray of golden sunlight found its way into the room and transformed the bag into something that just *had* to be magical. But he stopped himself from just grabbing the brown paper and emptying out its contents immediately. This was his birthday, and he wanted to cherish every second of it.

"Well?" said his mother between sips of tea. "Are you going to see what it is?"

He nodded dumbly. As he got up to look in the bag he noticed another smell, vying with the wide range of aromas that already filled the room. Leather? New shoes?

When he took the football out of the bag it seemed as though time stood still for a few seconds while he tried to take it all in. His eyes shone and his heart seemed to miss several beats. A lump filled his throat, rendering him speechless. He held the ball up to his face and breathed in the *newness* of it. He kissed it, squeezed it between the fingers of both hands - it was even fully pumped-up.

"Oh, *Mum!*" he squeaked eventually, holding the ball close to him and then holding it out again to view in case this was just a wonderful dream which would become yet another lost wish when he awoke. He hugged his mother, and was only just able to stifle tears of pure joy.

"Thank you! It's the best present I've ever had!" he said over his shoulder as he ran with it towards the front door.

"And where do you think *you're* going?" she called after him. He stopped at the foot of the stairs and chuckled. He was still wearing only his pyjama trousers and vest. He bounded upstairs to his room, threw on some clothes and two minutes later was heading for the park.

Chapter 3

When Paul reached the park he could see that his friend Jimmy was already there. Paul was overjoyed – though not entirely surprised – to find someone he could show his new football to; Jimmy was always at the park before any of the others and, he realized, was always the last to leave at the end of the day's play. Now he came to think about it, he had never seen Jimmy at school or anywhere else but here, and they had been kicking balls here for much longer than Paul could remember; practically every day. During blizzards, thunderstorms, hail and heatwave, Jimmy had always been here.

Despite Jimmy's diminutive stature, Paul couldn't recall any opposing striker ever running past him with the ball. With an economy of fuss, Jimmy had transformed countless attacks on their goal into counter-attacks and, true to the rest of his team mates' standards, he never committed a foul on anyone.

Jimmy got up from the wooden park bench when he saw his friend approaching, his smile broadening as he realized that they'd have a proper football to play with now. Paul jogged to the edge of the park and with his first kick, launched his new football high into the air with a right-footed goalkeeper clearance type of punt. The ball sailed through the summer morning sky as though in super slow motion, causing something of a protest among a few white gulls that had suffered a near miss and onto Jimmy's left instep - some fifty yards distant - where he caught it comfortably with both hands, the ball continuing to spin with momentum, even in his grasp. He squeezed it, grinned and called out to Paul, who was still some distance away.

"It's even fully pumped up!"

Paul returned the grin, the sweat from his sprint to the park already saturating him, and nodded. For a while they traded passes with this 'actual proper football'. Jimmy was clearly impressed, but said nothing as they both darted back and forth.

"Mum bought it for my birthday!" said Paul, picking it up, tossing it into the air and heading it to his friend. Jimmy headed it back.

"So how old are you now then?"

"Ten!" replied Paul, brightly. "You ten yet, Jimmy?" Paul

spun around to give the ball another huge hike into the atmosphere, so he didn't see his friend's expression darken momentarily.

"Oh yeah – couple o' weeks ago I turned ten" he said, catching the plummeting ball on his foot and pretending to weave and dodge with it between imaginary opponents, all the time keeping his face away from Paul.

"What did you have for your birthday, Jimmy?" panted Paul as he tried to become one of his friend's adversaries, chasing the jinking, ducking and ever-elusive boy. Though Jimmy was moving at speed and demonstrating highly athletic skills, his reply was quiet, nonchalant and offhand.

"Oh toys. Things. You know." Suddenly he stopped, picked up the ball and pointed off to the far side of the park. "Here come some of the others."

Despite having perfectly good vision, Paul was unable to see anyone at all.

"Where?"

"Between the two taller trees down there, towards the lake" insisted Jimmy and, before Paul could ask him *who* was approaching, he obliged:

"Dougie, Ron, Will and the Foxton twins." Jimmy was now scanning the ground beneath the shady canopy of a nearby tree. He noted the warning cackle of a pair of passing blackbirds and an odd smile crept across his face.

With considerable difficulty, Paul was, at last, able to

make out some tiny figures about a mile away. He looked back at Jimmy for a moment before returning his attention to the almost indiscernible group of children.

"Crikey!" said Paul. A few minutes went by before Paul was able to see for himself that it was Dougie, Ron, Will and indeed, the Foxton twins.

Chapter 4

Education in the period between the two World Wars in England, despite its shortcomings, imposed a set of values that its pupils would largely continue to maintain and nurture throughout their lives. There was still serious crime, but there were far fewer people around than today. There were not so many roads, and a fair percentage of the population tended to notice things that were out of the ordinary in the place where they lived and worked, so law and order were having a quiet cup of tea together down at the station for much of the time. With many honestly employed, and a set of standards regularly maintained with sweat and gritty toil by most of the populace, education failed only in that its limited fount of knowledge was still in its infancy.

Much of the schoolchild's lesson time was taken up with learning pounds, shillings and pence, cubits, fathoms, yards, feet and inches, furlongs and leagues. This left little time for foreign languages (apart from Latin) and spelling was often atrocious and unchecked.

Which brings us to Ron 'Snipper' Organs.

Ron's father, also called Ron, was the local veterinary surgeon. If you didn't want your dog to be capable of impregnating all the local bitches, you took him to Mr Organs for 'the snip'. His customers referred to him privately as 'Snipper' Organs, a nickname that became more popular than he was aware. To further complicate matters however, Ron Senior saw active military service as a marksman during the Great War (as it was then known) and was decorated with full honours as a 'Sniper, First Class'.

Ron Junior therefore, was constantly taught by his father that he was a 'chip off the old block'. Most of Ron Junior's spare time would be commandeered by his father to take him out shooting rabbits in the woods. Ron Senior would invariably bag a brace of bucks in the first foray, while Ron Junior would use his not-inconsiderable shooting skill to sever a single leaf above the quarry to give the doomed creature at least a head-start. Ron Junior didn't want to kill anything. Despite being a completely natural and alarmingly accurate marksman himself, Ron Junior only ever wanted to play football.

Ron Senior believed that football was a fine pursuit for any young lad – but if he wanted to go out and shoot rabbits in the woods, then young Ron would bloody well be there too until he became 'good enough' to bring home a kill of his own.

"Anyway," he would add, "You've got all the time in the world to play games, my lad. When you're old enough you'll be joinin' up."

Ron sighed inwardly. He didn't want to be a veterinary surgeon like his dad and he had no feelings at all about 'joinin' up' with the army. All he really craved was as much time as possible to play football with his friends. His dad would tell him that there were football matches played by soldiers regularly. "Good, healthy exercise. Team spirit and all that rot." he would say. Though young Ron didn't fully realize it yet, all he would really wish for was a 'normal' local occupation that would leave him plenty of time to play football with his mates.

Right now, he was barely nine years old and the summer holidays were still here. His dad was at his surgery, the sun was shining, he'd just had his breakfast and he was on his way out for a game.

As he turned the corner at the end of his street, he heard a familiar voice shout something unfamiliar.

"Snipper!"

Ron glanced around to see two boys running towards

him. Dougie Brown and Will Green lived next door to one another, a few streets further along from where Ron lived. Ron frowned in what he hoped would look like complete confusion.

Dougie and Will confronted him, an arm around the shoulder of the other, and began jigging up and down in a bizarre vaudevillean parody. Then, roughly in time with the jigging and trying to convey the volume of a crowd of football supporters on the terraces, they recited:

"S - N – I - P - E - R, *SNIPPER!*"

Ron watched as they practised their goal celebration manoeuvres, all the while breathing noisily out of their ecstatically open mouths to simulate the roar of a truly appreciative crowd. Eventually, they seemed to have exhausted their repertoire and contented themselves with practising their devastating '1-2' quick passing routine with a tennis ball that Dougie had 'borrowed' from his older sister.

Ron tried to follow the ball as the two eight-year-olds ran with it down the street, but it was so rapid as to be impossible. Trotting along behind he could see the occasional cloud of dust kick into the air above the road between them. His heart seemed to drum rapidly in his ears. Despite the evidence of his senses however, Ron was far from blowing a gasket. He wasn't even out of breath, so...?

The beating stopped, a flatbed truck clattered across the end of the street and the world became still and quiet.

Suddenly, he could see the tennis ball bouncing invitingly in his path.

"Snipper! Man on!" called Will from his left. The most natural thing in the world for Ron to do at that moment was, in fact, what he actually did. Completely in his stride, he looked directly down on the ball as it came down for another bounce and, with his left foot, sent the tennis ball hurtling towards the T-junction at the end of the street at slightly-below-the-crossbar height. Dougie and Will ran for cover.

When the ball connected with the sign on the lamppost, it severed the string at the top and sent it clattering into the gutter. The ball rebounded and, still travelling at speed, returned to Ron's hand.

Hidden in an alleyway, the three checked that the coast was clear before resuming their journey to the park. As they sauntered past the fallen sign, Ron looked to see what its message had been.

BALL GAMES PROHIBITED
<u>by order</u>

Twenty yards down the street they felt at ease enough to laugh quietly at the irony of their deed. Another fifty yards and their laughter became louder with the thrill of not having been found out. Then they heard a distinctly authoritarian-sounding voice yell: "OY!" from about a hundred yards behind them. They ran like hell.

Once they were safely around another three turnings into different streets the trio slowed their pace, smiling and saying hello to Billy, the rag and bone man, who happened along on his tatty old cart (with matching horse). Ron walked between Dougie and Will as they approached the Foxton twins' house.

"That's not how you spell 'Snipper', you know" said Ron.

Dougie considered this statement while Will celebrated having scored another imaginary goal. The twins' heads appeared from behind the hedge, wearing identical toothy grins and sporting freckles that seemed to intimate that the entity responsible for giving these girls their red hair had been clumsy with His or Her paintbrush.

Dougie saw the twins first and decided to see if the mirror-image six-year-olds could help settle the matter.

"Hello Julie –" he began.

"June!" corrected the one he'd been speaking to.

"Sorry! Hello June. How do you spell Snipper?"

As one, the girls gave a shrug. Being six years old, neither of them had much interest in words other than 'To June/Julie – Happy Christmas/Birthday from your

Auntie/Uncle/Mum/Dad/Nan/Grandad/Other'. If the words were attached to anything other than a gift for them, they were simply not interested. In later years they would both progress academically, but they were unable to conjure any enthusiasm for *any* pursuit normally associated with girls of their age. Their huge collections of dolls were gathering dust in their toy cupboard and their expensive matching toy prams had never been given an airing. They each had a teddy bear, but that was all, apart from a regular demand for a 'proper' football (which always fell on deaf ears. Both their mother and father had very strict views concerning young ladies playing football) the twins continued to receive 'girly' gifts, which would be dutifully unwrapped and discarded at the earliest opportunity. They were polite enough to avoid hurting the feelings of the relation supplying the gift, showing even a glimmer of appreciation as their minds rejected it out of hand.

The only gift able to strike a true spark of joy came by way of a rich uncle on their fifth birthday. The girls had opened the strangely cube-shaped boxes and gasped in delight. Their parents, taken aback by this genuine show of emotion, wondered what their uncle had found that was capable of producing such a rare event. Each girl lifted a netball from the wrappings and beamed at the other knowingly. Mr and Mrs Foxton however, realizing the danger signs, quickly stepped in to take the balls from their resisting hands. Father assumed his 'I'm-your-father-and-I-know-best' stance, the girls faces falling as they awaited the sermon.

"This," he said, holding one up and squinting at it, "is a hockey ball. Not for… *what?*" Their mother was prodding him. They watched her whisper in his ear and patiently waited for him to restart his speech.

"This," he said, holding one up and squinting at it, "is a *net*ball. Not for playing football with *at all*." He treated them both to individual searching stares and handed the balls back to them.

"Now *net*ball is a *wonderful* game for young ladies" he enthused imploringly. He glanced back at Mrs Foxton, who was lighting a cigarette. Sensing no resistance from his wife, he ploughed on.

"Maybe soon we can think about getting the rest of the equipment – nets, and proper netball bats – or is it racquets? – when you're a little older, of course."

Mrs Foxton choked noisily on her cigarette while the girls tried their level best not to burst out laughing. Unaware of his *faux pas*, their father began to reiterate his warning about the perils of playing football when, as one, the girls' left hands shot into the air.

"Toilet please, daddy!"

Mr Foxton looked back at his wife, whose tear-streaked face was convulsing in a superhuman effort not to explode with mirth.

"All right girls. Don't forget to wash your hands afterwards." Once the girls had left the room, Mr Foxton glared at his wife.

"You know, I really think you ought to pack in that filthy habit. It doesn't set a very good example to the girls, don't you think?"

Mrs Foxton watched her husband pack his favourite meerschaum with his usual pungent shag. Finishing her cigarette, she ground it out in the glass ashtray on the table next to her. The girls had spent ten minutes splashing loudly in the bathroom upstairs in order to mask their hysterical laughter.

Their main presents of the day, the expensive matching toy prams from their parents, were not presented for another hour. However, the controlled glee the girls normally held in reserve for ghastly girly gifts became uncontrollable as their every rehearsed 'Yes-it's-lovely-thank-you' dissolved into fits of giggles whenever their father's earlier speech was silently recalled.

From their front room window, Mr and Mrs Foxton watched the girls join the three older boys and set off. The park was only a short distance away, but the girls always insisted that the boys accompany them to 'protect' them. If either of their parents thought for one moment that the girls were playing football in the park, they would not have allowed them out at all. Whenever the twins were questioned about their activities afterwards, they would simply respond by saying that they had spent the day taking it in turns to push each other on the swings. In reality, the girls were earning themselves a reputation as a cutting-edge pair of dynamo midfield playmakers. They were considered good enough to play alongside the boys who comprised the rest of the team.

They positioned themselves each side of Ron and reached up to take a hand. Before setting off, the twins waved happily to the window where Mr and Mrs Foxton waved uncertainly back. Ron, glowing with embarrassment, set off after Dougie and Will, who were rehearsing their rapid-fire '1-2' routine with the tennis ball again. As the twin thuds of the ball that ricocheted from their boots receded into the distance, Ron realised that *that* had been the sound he'd earlier mistaken for his own heartbeat.

Chapter 5

Having assembled on one of the park's many full-sized football pitches, Dougie and Will were vying with Ron and the twins to inspect Paul's fine new birthday present. None of them had been anywhere near an actual *proper* football before. Nothing much was said as they grappled it from each other's grasp. Gasps and childish oaths were spontaneously loosed. Paul watched Jimmy dash among them and emerge with the ball somehow glued to his chest. A cry of protest went up, but Jimmy's expression, running with the ball still balanced on the front of his ragged, faded, short-sleeved shirt, indicated that he had not used his hands in performing the manoeuvre. Eventually, gravity came back into the equation and Jimmy was forced to maintain a complicated dance to keep possession as the three boys and the two little girls gave chase.

The arrival of Reg Wright and his father caught Paul's attention. Reg's father was none other than the Johnny Wright who had managed to get on Fulham's teamsheet regularly for two whole seasons. Unfortunately, those were the two seasons when the club had endured the most disastrous spell in its history. Having played as a supposed goal-scoring hero throughout every calamitous ninety minutes, he had failed to find the net once. Then, during the final moments of his career with Fulham, he had got his head in the way of a shot while tangled in the hectic frenzy of a goalmouth scramble. Johnny's goalkeeper, completely wrong-footed, could only stare in horror as the ball bobbled merrily over the line to nestle comfortably in the corner of the net.

His head still ringing from having intercepted a raking half-volley (which the goalkeeper had had covered anyway) Johnny Wright realised that he had opened his account with the team at this moment, albeit for the wrong side. The significance of what he had done was only just beginning to dawn on his central nervous system – which was otherwise engaged right then, due to the violent impact suffered by the side of his head. Only some thirty-five thousand other people knew that he had scored in his own net.

Thirty seconds later – just as Johnny had been starting to function normally again – the final whistle had blown.

His goal had been the only one of the game. If it hadn't been for the fact that Manchester United had just thrashed Bradford Park Avenue 11-0 elsewhere that afternoon, Fulham would have faced certain relegation. Johnny Wright, far from being a hot shot, was dropped from the team like a hot potato and never played professionally for anyone ever again.

Johnny still supported the club and would take Reg to see them now and then. Reg always wondered on these occasions why they always had loads of room in the stand when the rest of the ground was packed solid.

Reg was small, pudgy and bespectacled. At 11 he was the oldest member of the team, unless his father joined in to make up for someone delayed or unable to make it to the park for whatever reason. His father, sensing his son's eager yearnings to be a goalkeeper, had splashed out and bought him a pair of 'proper goalie gloves' during a visit to a sports outfitter's several birthdays previously. Despite the passing of time and the fact that he wore these same gloves to every game, they still looked brand new.

This was not because Reg was never tested; despite his uncanny and unlikely agility in the thick of the fray, he still let in the occasional goal. The gloves, however, always seemed to be somewhere else when the ball was screaming goalwards. His usual method of saving such a shot would involve jumping as high as possible with both arms raised to the sky, while the ball seemed to unerringly home in on the boy's head. The rebound would invariably go out for a throw-in, sometimes as far back as the centre line flag, while Reg would disentangle himself from the goal net, occasionally spitting blood. The others thought it small wonder that Reg's head was becoming more and more ball-shaped with every nose-flatteningly ferocious shot aimed at him. Reg would have been well served by trading his gloves for a helmet and a faceguard.

While they waited for their other four friends to arrive, Reg's father called everyone together to choose sides for their usual six-against-six kickabout. The Foxton twins always played on the same side during these games. Also inseparable were Dougie and Will. Johnny Wright glanced at his watch and turned around in time to see Terry, Robin, Thomas and Howard jogging toward them from the distance. "Ah" was all he had time to say. He had noticed the large group approaching at the same time.

Thomas Jones, the lanky welsh seven-year-old, had spoken to them last week about the group of bigger boys whose families had moved into the new housing estate, near the farm where Thomas lived. Shocked, the others had listened as the gangly Cardiff lad described the boys as answering back to their parents when being reprimanded for shattering another window with their careless kickabouts in their recently-created neighbourhood.

"Hello everyone!" said Thomas. "Remember I was telling you about those boys from the new estate last week?" The youngsters looked from him to the forbidding mob behind him. "Well this is them, and they say they want to play against us."

There was silence as the team looked to Mr Wright to give his grown-up stamp of approval to this proposition. Reg's father had also heard the tales of these bigger boys and their tough image. All he could think of to say, however, was: "erm..."

Before he was able to add to his speech, someone with a very powerful grip had seized his right hand and was pumping it violently up and down. A loud and brash voice brought up the rearguard of this surprise attack, making any interjection or objection impossible.

"Good day, sir! Bentley Sadfield at your service." The massively-whiskered, broad-shouldered, barrel-chested man carefully removed his black jacket, handing it absent-mindedly to a slightly smaller version of himself who stood beside him. He barely paused for breath and maintained the headlong momentum of his speech as he continued.

"We were supposed to be playing against Northfields this morning, but they gave us some rubbish about a funeral, so we're going to play against your lot instead, for a bit of practice." Mr Sadfield paused for a fraction of a second, gave Reg's father a few close looks and laughed in his face. Reg's father, his cheeks sprayed liberally with Mr Sadfield's saliva, cringed as he awaited the inevitable.

"Johnny Wright!" Bentley Sadfield spat the name as though it would conjure up some nasty creature from the nether world. Reg's father watched the cruel glee on the faces of Sadfield's team of ruffians as all the blood in his body seemed to be trying to exit from his cheeks and forehead.

"Heads or tails, Mr Ace Goalscorer?" said Sadfield, a lazy, unconcerned grin languishing across his visage. Johnny looked from the bigger boys to where this grown-up bully of a man was balancing a sixpenny piece on the nail of his thumb.

"Heads" ventured Johnny, uncomfortably. It was his first opportunity to speak since having had his hand crushed. Sadfield glanced at the coin and returned it to a pocket with a "hardluckit'stails" before anyone else had a chance to see. Then, choosing ends and kicking off practically immediately, Bentley Sadfield produced a whistle, declared himself referee and ordered Johnny Wright off the pitch.

Intensely humiliated, Johnny made his way towards a park bench where, burying his face in his hands, he knew that he would have to watch his son's team get taken apart by a bunch of young thugs, which was going to be even more humiliating. He would also have to explain to a lot of parents why their offspring were suddenly receiving hospital care. He chanced to look up and saw his son looking back at him from the goalmouth. Reg was smiling, his thumbs up, waiting for his father to return or acknowledge the gesture.

Johnny leaped from the bench and sprinted around the perimeter of the pitch to his son. He hugged him awkwardly and removed Reg's glasses, putting them carefully into his inside jacket pocket for safekeeping.

"Safe keeping, Reginald!" Reg had time to smile briefly and wave, turning to the action in time to receive a cannonball shot which rebounded from his forehead. He picked himself up, waved to his father and displayed the pristine thumbs of his gloves again.

Sadfield's younger version prepared to take the resultant throw-in near the halfway line. Sadfield senior, however, was blowing his whistle with a vengeance, indicating that he wanted play stopped. He ran over to where June and Julie were inspecting a small portion of the pitch with the air of kids in a rock pool at the seaside. Sadfield, his vast muscles rippling beneath the stretched fabric of his white collarless shirt, stood next to the twins, pointing at them, and continued to blow a long, piercing shriek that was beginning to add a headache to Johnny's list of woes. He wasn't sure he'd be able to bear seeing his son save another shot with his poor head again, either.

"Excuse me, but should these little girls *be* here?" said

Sadfield, with apparently genuine concern. June and Julie looked up at the towering figure with the muscles and the whistle and then, as if on a signal, they looked over to where Johnny writhed in torment on the bench.

Something inside Johnny snapped. He pulled himself together, strode purposefully over to Sadfield, held his gaze for a moment and said:

"Yes, they should be. Now, can we continue with the game, *please?*" Without waiting for a reply, Johnny Wright turned on his heel and strode back to the bench.

Sadfield glared at this outburst and, still looking daggers at Reg's father, inclined his head.

"Okay boys. Let's show 'em that we mean *business!*" He blew his whistle, stepped forward with a great air of drama, and fell over the twins. His whistle, slipping from his hands, spun end over end towards where the ball now was. Ron swiped at the ball and seemed to miskick it entirely. The ball bounced off the head of the now horizontal Mr Sadfield and was taken on by one of the bigger boys, whose average age was about fourteen.

As the boy ventured to run on to the ball, he could see the identical red-haired girls smoothing down the same patch of ground they had been investigating before the referee had blown up and fallen over. The boy began to realise that the piece of ground was exactly where the ball was going to be at any second. At the last moment, June stood up and calmly trapped the ball dead under her left foot. A split-second later Julie sent the ball flying forward with a smart, left-footed pass to where Dougie and Will stood poised, prepared to run with it down the right wing.

Sadfield was on his hands and knees, searching in vain for his whistle. Johnny Wright was feeling much improved, having spotted Ron's miskick for what it really was, and had managed to follow the initial part of the whistle's trajectory as it became a dwindling silver streak, cartwheeling inevitably toward the lake some distance away.

Dougie and Will ran the big boys' defence inside out. No one could tackle them, or even properly see which of them had the ball at any given moment. Eventually, Dougie was up-ended by a wild tackle, but he'd already fed it back out to Will, who quickly crossed it to where Ron approached the edge of the penalty area.

Sensing an opponent closing in from both sides, Ron took the shot early with his right foot, stopped dead and jumped smartly back a few feet. Once the older boys had finished colliding with each other in front of him and were in the process of falling over, Ron had the pleasure of seeing his shot ricochet into the net - via the goalkeeper's head and the crossbar.

Johnny spent the rest of the game in a state of profound wonderment. Countless times he watched, horrified, as a group of the older boys would – after a brief consultation with one another – decide to gang up on one of the youngsters, whether he had possession of the ball or not. After experiencing a sense of rage, combined with a cold sweat, Reg's father would, again, be on the verge of running across to intervene. The bigger boys tried it on with all the youngsters (except the girls) but could never land a single punch or kick. As usual, the twins' involvement with the play was minimal, but it always culminated in a particularly incisive throughball.

Occasionally, the older boys would try to tackle the player who was actually in possession at the time. But despite Bentley Sadfield's blatantly obvious and mysterious refereeing decisions, and the bully-boy tactics of his son's bigger and more physical team, Reg's first-minute 'save' was the only action he saw.

Sadfield senior, at the end of the ninety minutes, declared the match a close-run 0-0 draw. When Johnny Wright heard that, he clutched at his sides, collapsed to the ground and writhed on the grass. Sadfield saw him go down and began shepherding his exhausted team away.

"Well played, boys" he said as he led them off, still keeping his eyes peeled for his missing whistle. Reg and the others crouched down to see what was wrong with the still convulsing Johnny Wright.

"Dad? Are you all right, Dad?" Reg was getting tearful

now. Then his father turned his face and looked back at his son. He gasped breathlessly and gripped Reg's pudgy shoulders. Reg was beginning to wonder what he would have to do - his father being the only grown-up around. Who would phone for the ambulance?

After a lengthy coughing fit, several more gasps of air and another coughing fit, Johnny suddenly sprang to his feet. Though the children had survived the whole match by anticipating every vicious punch and kick aimed at them - *and* outplayed their larger opponents - they were, nevertheless, surprised by Reg's father's apparent ability to rise from the dead. They got to their feet and realised that he had merely been the victim of hysterical mirth. Judging by the quantity of tears on the man's cheeks and his rather alarming expression, they surmised that it must have been a good one.

"A close run nil-nil draw?" he was finally able to mutter, staring incredulously at the hotch-potch of children still assembled around him. He pointed at Ron, who pretended to flinch. "I saw Ron put at least seven past their keeper!"

Ron muttered something under his breath. Johnny leaned nearer to the boy.

"Sorry Ron. What was that?" Ron looked awkward as he repeated what he said.

"It was nine, actually" he confessed in a low voice.

Johnny laughed, pointing now at the sullen-looking six-year-old left-winger.

"Howard Gorman! Where's your pot of glue? How else could the ball stick so well to your feet? Nice hat-trick, by the way!"

The young boy flicked a long switch of black hair from his face and, failing to maintain his keen and aloof exterior, lapsed into an engaging grin. With that, Paul's new ball was suddenly at his feet and Jimmy was calling out the teams for the six-a-side kickabout they'd come here for in the first place.

Still grinning, Howard ran off with the ball towards the goal. One of the others laughed and shouted that he was going the wrong way.

Instantly, the crowd of youngsters chasing him stopped as he turned and weaved through them all; the ball seemed to travel in every direction but the anticipated one. Having beaten everyone on the team, Howard bore down on Reg, who was trying to make himself look big.

Howard could see that the goalkeeper had got his angles slightly wrong and steadied himself to despatch a shot to Reg's left. When the ball left Howard's right boot, he knew he had hit it much too hard. He knew Reg's habit of getting his head in the way and he didn't want to hurt his friend.

Luckily, the shot whistled just past Reg's left ear. Howard got ready to celebrate. However, the ball swerved at the last moment, cannoned into the post, came hurtling back out and rebounded off the top of Reg's head for a throw-in, up near the halfway line.

Johnny trotted around the pitch, watching the tireless and ever more complicated moves and intricate passing sequences being performed by this unlikely-looking group of footballers whose average age was eight. He never became too involved in these six-a-side skirmishes, though when he and his son had first begun making regular outings to the park a few years previously, Johnny, feeling himself to be a representative of the Professional Game, had taken it upon himself to 'coach' them. When he realized that the least skilful of them knew more about how to play football than he would ever truly be able to comprehend, he became more of an amazed spectator.

The ball went out to Dougie and Will on the right. Jimmy and the twins moved to close them down. Johnny listened to the rhythmic drumming of a frantic interchange of passes and marvelled at the amazing stamina of them all. Having the presence of mind to sidestep rapidly, he managed to avoid being caught up in the frenzied melée of one side's attack meeting the other's defence as it careered wildly around him. Ron fired a scorching volley and was already celebrating the goal when Reg flipped sideways and caught the ball with both hands.

"Well *done,* son! *Excellent* save!"

The attack was suddenly a counter-attack and Johnny

found himself almost completely alone. He watched as they streamed the length and breadth of what was, after all, a full-sized pitch. Despite their relatively small size, the children more than made up for any shortcomings by being twice as fast, twice as accurate and infinitely more dedicated than any of their grown-up contemporaries.

Added to that, he thought to himself as the play began to move back towards him again, they've just played a full ninety minutes against a team twice as big and twice as old as themselves.

He saw Ron thundering towards him with the ball and decided to head for the touchline.

Ron seemed to be well away until the twins appeared from nowhere. June just happened to be where the ball was, somehow, and she diverted it across to her sister. Julie took the ball first time and, with an economy of effort, volleyed it out to where Terry Pebworth caught it on his chest. Toddling along behind the rest of the action, the Foxton twins set out to provide extra cover, should this counter-offensive that they had just engineered break down.

Johnny Wright sat on the bench to watch the rest of their game, trying to remember exactly how many goals (all wrongly disallowed) they had beaten the older boys by. He got up to seventeen before giving up.

Chapter 6

MONDAY, 17TH APRIL, 1962 AD

Robert Carlton lay in his bed, listening to the rain pattering at the window. Knowing it was a Monday morning and that his two brothers would be getting drenched on their way to school gave birth to a physical feeling of satisfaction that rose from his abdomen and into his chest. By rapidly twisting himself from where he had been propped up on his pillow, he managed to project the feeling into a galvanized bucket that sat on the floor next to the bed. Opening his streaming eyes only to ensure that he'd hit the target, he wiped his face with some toilet paper from a roll nearby and resumed his previous position. His stomach hurt bad and he was hungry, but he couldn't even bring himself to look at the toast his mother had brought up for him earlier and had only sipped a little from the hot, sweet tea.

The doctor had called that morning and told him that he had a very dicky tummy, hadn't he, and that he was to take this medicine – even though it tasted the way he imagined plaster of Paris would taste – until it was all gone. Robert recalled his earlier appraisal of the bottle as it was produced and used to provide him with the first dose of the vile stuff. The bottle was huge, its green glass dark and foreboding, and it had Robert's name written on the white label in the doctor's curious script. He never did find out what colour the medicine was, because at every dose it was down to his mother to get it into the spoon and his mouth while the boy bunched his facial features into a grimace like a frozen, silent wail, his eyes tightly shut. As he swallowed, his eyes would open wide in horror and glare accusingly at his mother while she would stare back with deep, maternal concern, her hands replacing the top to the bottle with a graceful and natural dexterity.

After a few minutes of recovering from contributing another 'feeling' to mingle with its fellows in the bucket, Robert opened his eyes and gave vent to a sudden and unexpected burp. It smelled and tasted foul.

Just as he was waving his hands to waft the odour away, his mother burst into the room.

"What in God's name was that? Are you all right

Robert?" His mother's voice was high and quavering with worry, as she had been outside the front door when she'd heard the noise. The sound had carried right through the house and had caused her to almost fall over in her haste to finish putting the dustbin out and rush back up to his room.

"I'm all ri – *bleeugh!*" Another loud burp cut him short, bringing another quiet groan from the woman. Robert leaned away from her and did the wafting thing with his hands again. Once the foetid wind had been shown the window by his incredulous mother (she had never smelled anything quite so awful, either) Robert did, indeed, feel a lot better. He told her that he'd quite like to come down and have a light lunch a little later but, taking the doctor's advice to the letter, Robert was told, firmly, to stay in bed the whole week.

She brought him a delicious cheese and tomato sandwich which he wanted to devour immediately. As solid and as holy as a cathedral, Mrs Carlton painstakingly fed him the sandwich in small pieces, patiently ensuring that he chewed and swallowed it slowly.

Robert wanted another cup of tea but was given water, which he had been made to promise to drink slowly. He looked up at his mother as she got up from the edge of the bed. The sandwich had taken fifteen minutes to eat, yet this big, proud woman had sat there all the while, uncomplainingly feeding it to him.

They kissed each other on the cheek and he watched her leave the room, automatically picking up various shirts and socks from his brothers' beds for washing on her way out. Savouring the sweet scent of his mother's perfume, which masked his earlier rancid burps and seemed to epitomise safety and security, he slid back under the blankets.

Just as he was deciding that he would get up in a few moments, he fell into a sudden and deep sleep. He felt himself floating in total darkness. The rain on the window increased its ferocity and a bellow of approaching thunder reverberated around the room, but Robert was aware of none of it. He was in the park, watching himself and his friends playing football. He could see Phil Donaldson heading the ball away from an in-swinging corner kick. Then he saw himself bear down on the half-cleared ball, his body twisting and twitching as the dark youngster, shaping himself for a cannonball shot, feinted to his left, put the ball to his right and was thus past the first defender. Robert grinned in his sleep, watching himself wriggle through the crowded penalty area with the ball never more than an inch from either of his dancing feet. He recalled the time when his brothers (who had limited interest in the sport) had watched him at the park one day when they had been playing against some older boys. He had played a blinder, scoring seven goals, and even his siblings had to grudgingly admit that he had played 'quite well'.

But something was not quite right here, he thought to himself. He took a closer look at his friends in the goalmouth scramble. None of them were wearing their usual clothes and, now that he was paying more attention to the detail in this highly-realistic dream, he found that he couldn't really properly identify *any* of them. Their characteristics were all there and their general shape, but the faces were wrong. Robert couldn't believe that they could play so much like himself and his usual friends and yet *not* actually *be* them.

He watched himself get up from having been tackled, practically on the goal-line, by someone who looked exactly like Jimmy York, and who was now running straight towards where Robert's dream-self lingered on the side touchline.

Robert frowned as he looked at what should have been his own face on the boy who was being helped to his feet in the six yard box. Black though the youngster was, it wasn't *his* face, he was certain. Then he turned his attention to the boy they had nicknamed 'Hawk' and realised that of all the players there, Jimmy was the only one he'd been properly able to recognize. Also, it seemed that Jimmy could see him, too. He watched the boy come nearer and set his features to call out to Robert, but patches of strange, dark mist were flickering between them.

One of the misty patches dispossessed Jimmy and

swirled down the wing with the ball. Jimmy, treating the tackle with minor contempt, shook his head and, before he could vocalise his greeting to Robert, something heavy and lumpy connecting with his back tore him savagely away from the dream. The park, Jimmy and the not-quite-strangers vanished in a brief flurry of panic as Robert sought to defend himself from this sudden assault with arms that were numb from having been slept on.

When the other slightly smaller person jumped on him, he realized at once that his brothers were home from school and would now give him a hard time for having been in bed all day.

"Lazy mon!" said Roy, his older brother by a few years, his arms under the bedcovers, his fingers poking and tickling.

"*Sick* mon!" corrected Robert as he pushed his younger brother, Rupert, from where he had managed to perch with his knees across Robert's still-painful abdomen. Rupert landed with a loud crash among a pile of his own toys in the corner on the floor. The tickling and poking momentarily forgotten, they looked down at their brother, who was lying awkwardly across the battered remains of a broken wooden fort. There was a moment of silence, broken only by their mother's voice calling for them to cut it out.

Then Rupert calmly opened his eyes, looked up at the ceiling in a worldly way and said, "You missed a great day at school today."

Robert and Roy grinned at each other with immense relief. Robert had already been silently rehearsing what he was going to have to tell the policeman when he came to find out how he had killed his brother.

"Did I?" said Robert, glad that his brother had not, after all, suffered a fatal broken neck as a result of his fall. Rupert got up from the floor, removed a small part of a lookout tower from his ear and casually flung it into the almost completely destroyed fort that lay, desolate among the toy trucks and comics - the scene of at least one battle too many. He sat on the edge of the bed and pulled one of his funny faces at them.

"No," he said. "I made that bit up."

Suddenly their mother sailed into the room, aiming half-hearted swipes at her errant sons.

"I *tol'* you to *get* into that *bath*room and *wash* your*selves* and *leave* this *sick child alone!*" She punctuated her speech with the slaps, though none of them were intended to strike home. The last one did, in fact, connect with Rupert's head. Before he was even aware he'd been struck - though hardly severely - his mother had snatched him into her copious bosom and was hugging him almost to the point of suffocation, tenderly kissing the spot where she had made contact.

While Rupert endured this spontaneous outburst of enfolding adoration, Roy, being much more nimble, had avoided the swinging arms and was now in front of the bathroom sink, looking down at the spreading dark patch over the front of his trousers. He had rather carelessly turned the tap fully on and the freezing water had scooted over his palms and escaped the ceramic bowl.

Shepherding her youngest son from the room, Robert's mother looked back at him over her shoulder and promised to bring him something to eat soon. As she closed the door softly behind her, Robert could hear sounds of minor pandemonium erupt from the bathroom. Roy was being chastised for soaking his school trousers.

Robert pulled the bedding back into some kind of order and began to recall the dream. The rain was beating at the window again, though he'd slept soundly through the worst of the stormy weather. He slipped back under the blankets and closed his eyes tightly. The dream had him intrigued, but he could not get himself back there. He just wasn't sleepy enough any more.

Chapter 7

Mr Foxton puffed thoughtfully on his pipe, the smoke filling the sunbeams in the hallway with a substance all of their own. Long after he had strolled, somewhat theatrically, into the living room of the spacious semi-detached suburban house, the afternoon sunlight that streamed through the stained glass panels of the front door continued to writhe in long, slanted diadems of gold. Out of a sense of habit, Mr Foxton found himself positioned in front of the fireplace in a posture which, had he not regained consciousness of his actions, normally presaged a launch into yet another lecture for the benefit of his young twin daughters on how little girls should take more of an interest in dolls, prams and the like. He would then have added that football was, as always, strictly prohibited.

As it was, he aborted the vocal launch just before he'd begun addressing the two girls, who weren't there to receive it anyway, and took a stroll to the window that opened onto the back garden. Perceiving himself to be a man of culture, he had taken his wife to see plays at the local theatre. They would always dress to the nines on these occasions, Mr Foxton paying close scrutiny to the jargon and the dress sense of the other punters. He often tried to imitate those who seemed to fit his almost childish ideal, with embarrassing results, usually. The stroll he was currently trying to perfect had come from watching an extremely distinguished-looking gentleman at an evening of Shakespeare; he had seen the man wandering nonchalantly around the stalls during one of the intervals. Mr Foxton was so impressed with the man's unusual gait that he promised himself to begin practising it as soon as that evening's programme was concluded.

(In fact, unknown to Mr Foxton, the man with the impressive way of walking was a confidence trickster with a stolen painting rolled up and concealed within a tube strapped to his right leg. The distinguished-looking gentleman had dived through the front-of-house doors to evade the police. If Mr Foxton had wanted to truly perfect this latest affectation, he would have been well-served by tying a broom handle to his leg.)

Still reminiscing deeply about this particular night at

the theatre, it took him a while for his eyes (and, eventually, his mind) to focus on what he was seeing in the garden.

With tiny and careful little movements, his daughters were placing scores of their dolls in a line along the edge of the garden. Some of the dolls leaned against old shoeboxes or upturned plant pots, on which would be placed more dolls. One of their prams gleamed in the late summer sunshine, further down the garden towards the pond. Mr Foxton, his mind now absorbed in this idyllic scene, smiled with relief. Maybe his lectures had not been falling on deaf ears after all.

With the girls' innocent giggling ringing in his ears and forgetting to even practise his new stroll again, Mr Foxton hurried to the stairs. His wife was in their bedroom putting clothes away when, smiling in a way she had not seen for more than ten years, Mr Foxton appeared at the door and beckoned her to follow him.

They descended the stairs quietly and without speaking until they both stood at the window, looking out at their daughters.

Mr Foxton was about to point out that the girls were, at last, taking an interest in more feminine pursuits, when their attention was drawn by a sudden blur of movement. June, crouched on the ground before the near end of the row of dolls, seemed to her mother to be asking one of them if it would like a nice cup of tea.

Her mother gasped with horror as she watched the girl spring into a standing spin and swing her tiny foot towards the neck of the end doll on the top tier. With a neat snap and a thud the doll's head sailed down the garden, where Julie's right foot connected with it in a perfectly-timed overhead scissor-kick. The severed doll's head hit the inside of the hood at the end of the pram and made the carriage roll back slightly. Before the momentum had time to run down, the second head was thudding into the hood. This one exhibited macabre signs of life by joining the first head and rolling around the inside of the gradually-accelerating toy pram.

By the time Mr and Mrs Foxton had run to the back door, every doll had been decapitated. The force of the last volley had propelled the pram inexorably in the direction of the pond where, after one of the wheels had chipped off the nose of a plaster gnome, it had tipped completely upside down and dumped its sinister cargo into the water.

Mr Foxton strode over to the girls and stood working his eyebrows at them in what he assumed would be interpreted as a 'grave manner'. But the twins were paying him no attention whatsoever. In fact, as he opened his mouth to chastise them, they ran either side of him towards the house.

His eyebrows began to take on lives of their own as he whirled around, ready to pursue his errant offspring. It was then that he noticed, with a deep sense of shock, that his wife – normally so self-assured and unflappable - was weeping. The girls were at her knees, offloading their own tears into the scented cotton of their mother's dress. In a strange and uncustomary show of affection, Mrs Foxton bent her knees and put an arm around each of the girls, drawing them in for a hug.

Without prompting, both girls solemnly swore that they'd never do that to the dolls ever again. Mr Foxton was now preparing to banish them to their room, but his preparations were for nothing. The tears had worn them out, and minutes later they were both asleep.

While their mother kissed their identical foreheads and tucked them into their beds, Mr Foxton was removing the pram from the pond and wondering at the sudden display of emotion from his wife. He looked down into the murky water to see nearly three dozen tiny faces looking back at him from the mud and the algae. One of the heads had managed to land, the right way up, on a lily pad, making it appear to be sporting a green Elizabethan ruff. He fished the heads out, emptied the water from every neck and put the heads back into the pram. Then he bundled the headless dolls into the pram with their various heads all rolling around separately and pushed the carriage into a dusty corner of the shed. On his way back across the garden to the house, he remembered to practise the stroll again.

Mrs Foxton, her eyes still puffy and wet, watched him from the girls' bedroom window, wondering what her husband might have injured that could possibly be causing him to walk in such a bizarre fashion.

Chapter 8

Jimmy York is not his real name. In 1935 he claims to be 10 years old, though this is not true, either. The others in the team all accept him for what he appears to be – a boy aged about ten, who is always the first to arrive for a game of football. The others don't seem to notice that he is the last to leave, too. They just accept him because, like the others, his skill is exceptional and he plays the central defender's role with aplomb.

He has never spoken of parents, nor where he might live. He does not like lying to his friends, but he knows there is no way he could explain his true age to them in a way that they would be properly able to understand. He has also never explained to any of his friends why they all immediately hit it off with each other or why they all feel as though they've known each other for much longer than would be possible, given their youthful age.

Jimmy cannot remember his original name; he has a vague memory of changing it (not for the first time) to James, which he first read from a monk's illumination of a gospel several hundred years before. York eventually became his adopted surname because he'd arrived in England on a merchant vessel at what was to become Scarborough and settled, for a time, in York. When he first arrived there, the town's name was in the process of being changed from the Roman Eboracum to the Danish Jorvik.

He can dimly remember Morten, the kindly Danish merchant who took him under his wing and transported him to this island, though many of the details of the adventure are hazy after a thousand years. Being immortal, Jimmy will always appear to be a normal ten-year-old boy. Normal, that is, unless you happen to catch a glimpse of his eyes. His skin and tousled brown hair both seem to lend credence to the little boy image. But a glance into his hawk-like eyes would reveal an eternity of experience far in excess of any ordinary mortal. Being cognizant of this, Jimmy is careful not to hold anyone's gaze for too long.

Several times throughout his incredibly long life, he has accidentally aroused suspicion among the people he has come in contact with. Sometimes, someone who had played with Jimmy as a child would see him again, much later in life. The child would now be approaching late middle age, while Jimmy would still appear to be exactly the same ten-year-old child from half a century before. Many times, Jimmy would have to move on to another part of the country when his current 'foster parents' began to notice that the passing of time was having no effect whatsoever on their 'little boy'.

Throughout the millennia, Jimmy has enjoyed the same circle of friends. These friends of his are not immortal in the same way that Jimmy is. Their bodies, being mortal, have only a normal life expectancy, while their spirits are joined forever in a 'Group Soul'.

Jimmy's friends are born, grow up a little, meet Jimmy and the others for the 'first' time and play football together until something happens which breaks the friends apart. Sometimes, the youths become drawn into a war and get killed. Except, of course, for Jimmy.

Jimmy will maybe move on to avoid having to explain why he still looks like a little boy when his friends all grow up past him. Then, once his friends have died, he'll wait for them all to be reincarnated so that they, unknowingly, can continue the game they thought they were just starting.

Chapter 9

When World War Two began, Ron Organs was 13 years old. His father had been recalled to his former regiment and on his first day back, had been killed by a stray bullet from a practice range. Ron junior was horrified when he heard of his father's death; outwardly he was calm and stalwart for his mother on the day of the full military funeral, but inwardly he blamed all Germans and Adolf Hitler in particular for luring his father into mortal danger, and was intent on signing up before he was old enough.

At nearly fourteen, his height, his wiry muscles and his air of quiet bravado convinced the Army that he was almost seventeen. His mother, never the same after her husband's demise, had sought solace in a gin bottle and was completely unaware when her only child joined up.

Ron wrote to her from his barracks a week after

signing up, explaining what he had done and why, but through a cruel act of fate the letter never arrived. A drunken postal worker had been driving the van and had lost control at a remote bend in the road. His feet slipped from the pedals while his hands clawed ineffectively at the wheel. The van careered sideways into the bend, flipped over and landed upside down in a deep, water-filled ditch. The inebriated driver had been killed instantly, his neck being broken and his skull crushed in the initial impact with the side of the road. The letter, among a big bag of others, rotted gently in the sack along with the driver and everything else in the van, which now lay the wrong way up, submerged by the quiet ditch.

Alone now, the newly-widowed Mrs Organs seemed to have also lost her only child during her period of mourning. The few personal friends she'd had were scattered by this ghastly war and, as she drank the days away, she became a frail recluse. Spending the last two weeks of her life completely alone, she eventually succumbed to malnutrition and dehydration.

Ron threw himself whole-heartedly into being an ideal soldier. He trained hard and, naturally, excelled on the rifle range. He had made many friends among his comrades-in-arms, had shone in their football team and could mix it with the best of them. No one called him 'Snipper' anymore.

He had not discussed his intention to join the army with any of his friends at the park, his father's death instilling in him an instant and overwhelming certainty that he had to join up as soon as was possible. Ron had not heard of his father's death until he had returned from what turned out to be his last game, to find his mother, unconscious and reeking of gin, sprawled in an armchair which had been turned to face the wall. He had covered her with a blanket and sat down to read the already-opened telegram.

The following week, Ron stayed with his mother and jumped with her at the funeral as the twenty-one gun salute was impeccably executed. The next day, he slipped out early with a few possessions wrapped in a knotted tablecloth. At the same moment that he signed his name in the enrolment building, Mrs Organs was struggling home with a loaf of bread and several bottles from the shop, convinced that her son would be back home from the park soon for his tea. Ron, however, was marching off to war, convinced that his mother would be capable of looking after herself while he went and found Adolf Hitler and shot him dead, thus laying his father's ghost to rest.

The war took the others to different parts of the globe; the matches were temporarily discontinued. Just one figure stayed at the park, practising and honing his unique football skills. His knees were muddy, his shirt and shorts old and torn, his hair a shock of dark brown that flicked across his brow as his head moved in a counterpoint rhythm to the movement of the ball on the ground. His hawk-like gaze would take in every detail of the surrounding greenery, reading the gesturing branches and the scattering of the clouds, knowing now that he would have to wait for a new team to be born and grow. Jimmy York flicked the ball up to the level of his waist, smiled sadly, then hiked the ball high into the atmosphere with his right foot.

Ron, who now insisted that his comrades call him 'Snipper', became as capable a marksman as his father had been before him, distinguishing himself in several conflicts and providing the others in his regiment with a living lucky talisman. When the going got rough, as long as 'Snipper' was with them, they knew that they would all survive.

And they always did. In fact, this held true right up to the evening when they stumbled upon an unexploded Allied bomb in enemy-occupied territory. Seeking shelter from driving, heavy rain and gale-force winds, Ron and his unit filed into the bomb-damaged warehouse. Ron was one of the first to enter the damp and gloomy building, exploring the vast, echoing walls with the beam from his torch. A ragged hole near the centre of the roof caught his attention, his torchlight illuminating the rain as it cascaded in. More of his men were pouring in through the door, so Ron moved further in to give them more room. Many of them were already finding a dry patch of floor to lie down on, exhaustion forcing them to make do with rough boards. The warehouse was becoming more crowded, so Ron only found the hole in the floor by almost falling into it. At the last instant, he threw himself to one side. He felt the floor give slightly, but significantly, under his weight when he landed.

"Fire in the hole!" he screamed as he struggled to regain his feet. Several of the last soldiers to come in heard the call and ran straight back out into the night, others falling in behind them. As he avoided the hole, Ron glimpsed what had caused it. All in one brief instant of time he realised that a bomb had fallen through the roof, impacting with the soil beneath the floorboards, and that the combined weight of the soldiers stumbling in the gloom would cause the rest of the floor to collapse and the bomb to detonate. He got as far as opening his mouth to shout another warning, but the explosion cut him short. The last thing he saw was a bright, blinding flash that seemed to go on forever.

Ron noticed that he no longer felt cold or wet, but his eyes were taking an eternity to grow accustomed to the brilliant light. Then he supposed he had been asleep, because he was now aware of being inside something with smooth walls that glowed slightly.

After another length of time he began to seek a way out from this strange and tiny room, though there was no sign of a door. Hunger and desperation eventually drove him to peck at the wall, which he began to gulp down greedily. Then it was light again. Ron looked at what he could see of himself and noticed that he was on the roof of a building, far from where he expected to be. Also, he had physically changed – quite a lot.

He opened his beak and croaked pathetically.

Chapter 10

So much of the planet has altered beyond what we, the children of the Third Millennium, would be able to recognize. More empires have risen and fallen; disastrous wars have been waged, with the usual dire consequences; plagues and famines have ravaged entire continents, killing billions; scores of ghastly atrocities have continued to be inflicted on the innocent and defenceless in the name of as many gods; savage tyrants have come to power and left their mark on the planet in the form of a ragged wound - leaving a telling and ugly scar of monstrous proportions - physically and spiritually; incredible inventions have astonished generations with their ingenuity.

Many of our descendants would agree that the Holographic Reciprocating Modulation Transmogrifier was one of the better ideas. Basically, it was a huge, three-dimensional video recorder/player, usually set up in a sports stadium. Football, being one of the few sports we would still be able to recognize (having been suddenly thrust three hundred years into the future) adopted the HRMT (or Hermit, as it became known), using it for life-size action replays when investigating off-the-ball incidents and the like. The HRMT was applied to all kinds of entertainment, educational purposes and, when it became more affordable, people could sit in their private recreation space and rent anything from a Shakespeare play to a miniature Star Wars epic to watch from different angles, again and again.

In fact, football was one of the first sports to seize on the invention in its early days. Pioneering its possibilities, a football match was played between Premiership heavyweights Bristol Rovers and First Division hopefuls Welwyn Garden City Wanderers. It was a third-round tie in the FA Cup and the new Eastville Stadium was crammed full with excited and expectant fans. With scores of white-coated technicians running around the perimeter of the pitch, the officials had their work cut out for them. If they made a wrong decision, they were aware that the run of play could be 'rewound' and scrutinized by all.

The players ran onto the pitch, but straight away the problems were obvious. Their pre-game warm-up became farcical when a player kicked a ball to a team mate who turned out to be nothing more than a spontaneously-generated image, still lingering in its original position on the part of the pitch where it had been recorded. The referee entered into a heated debate with a posse of technicians on the touchline, while the field behind him continued to proliferate with players, all displaying various frozen expressions of bafflement. To add to the confusion, a black mongrel ran into the centre circle. Some of the players began trying to catch it, but as the animal itself became subject to holographic recording and playback, the players found themselves grasping at thin air disguised as slightly flickering ghost images. Other players fell over as they discovered that the ball they had just swiped at ineffectually was only a holographic image.

The crowd were loving every minute of it, but the referee was threatening to abandon the game before it had even started. More technicians appeared around the referee. The two linesmen ran across to lend moral support and, as mild pushing and shoving ensued, the television commentator remarked, "Nobody likes to see that!"

A policeman intervened, his helmet falling off and rolling onto the field of play, where it became a whole row of helmets. By this time the players almost outnumbered the capacity crowd, the black dog was everywhere and the ticket-holders were laughing hysterically.

Twenty minutes late, the referee reluctantly called the

players back out to at least attempt to begin the game. The sound system, which until this moment, had not been working at all, suddenly burst into life as the irate referee blew his whistle. The sensitive equipment reproduced it as "WOOF!"

But the game was under way, the referee told himself, shaking his head and stumbling as he caught sight of a black dog as it appeared from behind him. He swung his foot at it irritably and fell over when he failed to make physical contact. The crowd were screaming and hooting with laughter still, but it was imperative that the game should go ahead. Even the HRMT's sternest critics could see its potential, so the players stuck to their task, doing their best to ignore the occasional black dog which would run backwards at high speed across their field of vision when they were sizing up a cross into the penalty area, or a crucial back-pass to the goalie.

As the game went on, the dogs became fewer and the white-coated technicians less agitated. By half-time, the crowd were discussing Rovers' four goal lead and everything seemed more like a normal football match at last. The game itself was exciting and close-fought – despite the seven-nil final scoreline – and the crowd went home with jaws still aching from the hilarious introduction to this new technology.

But they enjoyed it. Indeed, they went back the next

day and paid to see the whole match again, and again the day after that, crowding into the areas of the stands where they knew they'd have the best view of all the goals - which were, after all, guaranteed. The HRMT was now a reality, though it still faced a decade of uncertainty as its dimly-understood hardware went through its often-embarrassing teething problems.

Chapter 11

Ron found himself popular among his contemporaries; as a seagull, his sense of fun was suddenly increased a thousandfold, with the ether and the world below it his playground. He found that he was able to direct his faeces with incredible accuracy at a staggering range and his singing was the worst any other of his fellows had ever heard (an advantage in the seagull equivalent of etiquette, such as it was). But he was never far from the park, where he would watch the new incarnation of the youngsters playing football, cajoling and singing at them as they raced to and fro, far below him.

When they met up to choose sides before each game, Ron the seagull would come as close as he dared to the group of players, knowing he would never get picked but drawn to the game like a magnet.

In later years, shortly after the end of the Second World War, Ron saw the youngsters all progress into the same local professional team where, lacking only a sharp-shooting centre forward, they became hugely successful. Ron the seagull never missed even a kick-around when the boys got together.

Now they were in the fifth round of the FA Cup, drawn at home to Preston North End, who were generally assumed to be the eventual holders of the trophy at the end of the season. Every man and his dog knew this for a fact, so the young men trotted out cheerfully enough on the day, determined to at least enjoy the country's most skilful side in action, instructed by their manager to just do their best and have fun.

The sun was shining down from a cloudless sky as Ron took up his position on the roof of the stand behind the home team's goal. Some of the away fans were throwing things onto the pitch. Ron's acute vision immediately detected the instigator and he nonchalantly pushed away into the air. Utilising the accumulated heat from the packed stadium, he rose effortlessly to almost three hundred feet, where he unleashed a long, streaming projectile of seagull-poo.

Far below, the man directing the bottle-throwing was pulling a whiskey bottle from his pocket, draining its contents and readying himself to orchestrate another volley of rubbish onto the pitch. Feeling completely drunk, he threw his head back to belch loudly and add his own contribution to the broken glass already on the pitch. However, Ron's aim was true, and the ghastly muck flew straight down the man's exposed gullet at quite a lick. The man slumped sideways into the terracing, where he lay vomiting quietly for the rest of the game's duration. Deprived of their loutish ringleader, the would-be bottle-throwers decided to watch the match instead.

The game was tightly-contested. In fact, the home team could have been three up by half-time, but their centre-forward was having a bad day. Ron watched them run out to start the second half and fretted as his boys soaked up a long spell of pressure.

And then it happened.

A frantic goalmouth scramble had ensued after a series of Preston corners, and the centre-forward, back to help out in his own penalty area, had handled the ball. Both linesmen's flags went up and the referee blew his whistle simultaneously. Nobody argued about it, least of all the centre-forward himself, who hung his head and walked slowly towards the centre circle.

The Preston striker stepped up to take the shot. He wasn't at all nervous, because he had scored every penalty he'd ever taken at professional level. He was grinning confidently at the home side's goalkeeper as he prepared to run up to the ball. Everyone was in position and an expectant hush descended over the stadium. Ron waited on the roof behind the goal, saw the striker begin his run-up and began a high-speed dive. In the split-second before his foot could make contact with the ball, a piercing shriek assaulted his ears and upset his balance by just enough for his resultant scuffed shot to roll slowly towards the goalkeeper. Having been poised to deflect a thunderbolt, the goalie dived onto the ball dramatically, though it had almost come to a halt by then.

When Ron had unleashed the cannonade of sound, he had been hurtling straight at the striker and had directed it, with some force, into his ears. The referee whistled for the kick to be retaken and Ron forced himself to watch from the stand roof as the striker took his second attempt.

The Preston player hit it hard, aiming for the centre of the goal, which all the other goalkeepers had conveniently vacated by opting to dive one way or the other. This goalkeeper, however, never did that kind of thing. This goalkeeper knew that the best method was letting the ball come to him, rather than diving inadvertently out of its path. Consequently, when the ball rocketed towards his face, he simply caught it in both hands and, without waiting to be congratulated by any of his team mates, ran past the crestfallen penalty-taker and hoofed the ball downfield.

Spurred on by this change of fortune, the home team broke out to form a long series of attacks which, had they had a competent enough centre forward, would have culminated in a glut of elegantly-worked goals. The atmosphere became more intense as the game edged, still goalless, into its final few minutes.

Then, when it seemed that the game would have to be replayed up north, the home team were awarded a direct free kick, just outside Preston's penalty area. Ron flapped around his boys and settled on the ground near the ball. As the referee signalled for the kick to be taken, the gull cocked its head in a way that struck a chord with the home team player running up to take the shot. Ron took off and flew over the wall of defenders as the kick was taken.

When the ball came over the wall and struck Ron, he knew he would never recover from the shattered bones and the broken wing that the ball had inflicted on him. But before he hit the ground, he had the pleasure of seeing his deflection creep underneath the crossbar and snuggle into the corner of the net. The referee blew to confirm the goal and then again a few seconds later to signal the end of the match. The Preston players converged angrily on the officials who were doing their best to get off the pitch, while the home team players went to where their unlikely match-winner lay in a white blanket of feathers at the edge of the six-yard box.

Tenderly, they picked up his dying body and, seeing the creature was doomed anyway, took him on a lap of honour around the pitch, displaying the bird to the jubilant home supporters before plying Ron with strong spirits to send him happily into the after-life. They had a whip-round and paid a taxidermist to stuff Ron, whose body still stands proudly atop the match ball in the club's trophy room.

Chapter 12

25TH OF MARCH, 1205 AD

Jimmy had spent the previous night in the snug interior of a hay barn, listening to the storm hammer on the roof as he shared his shelter with a mixture of birds, rats and mice, all co-existing uneasily for the duration of the howling wind and the relentless rain. When the farmer came out at sunrise to shoo the creatures out into the steady drizzle that the storm had become, Jimmy had already gone.

Continuing to head south, Jimmy followed the ancient track as it negotiated great, rolling dales and densely-wooded valleys when, cresting a hill, he caught sight of the forest. He stopped to survey its expanse, turning his whole body through one hundred and eighty degrees to take in its nearest edge. From his viewpoint on the hill he was able to cast his gaze above its perimeter and see the lush blanket in a thousand different shades of green as it replicated the contours it sprang from. Jimmy walked down the slope, noting that the track would lead him straight into the thick of it. The rain, still a steady downpour, saturated the grey sackcloth smock which he wore, tied at the waist with a plaited leather belt. His ragged brown cloak was plastered to his shoulders as he aimed for the promise of shelter beneath the trees.

The rain began to beat down more heavily, and Jimmy increased his pace. When he reached the forest, a sudden and vicious hailstorm joined in the fun. Standing with his back against the bole of a great elm, he watched the huge white snowball-sized globes of ice bounce past him to form a living carpet that poured along the track, well into the forest. The sun made a fleeting appearance and briefly painted the scene with the colours of a thousand rainbows. Jimmy drank in the beauty of it until the sun disappeared again and a cold wind blew down the track. He shivered in his dripping clothing and looked back out of the forest.

The ground was a uniform white, concealed beneath the coating of colossal hailstones. Hoisting his bag over his shoulder, Jimmy picked his way carefully along the track until he had passed the last of the melting chunks of ice. He turned to look back at the forest entrance and was again treated to another brief flickering of sunshine, with its attendant rainbow. The clouds broke the spell as before and Jimmy carried on, enjoying the protection the trees afforded him from the monotonous rain that had drummed at him all morning.

Jimmy followed the track for a few miles without meeting another living soul, until he sensed that someone was watching him from a fair distance away. He paused briefly to examine the ground below a horse-chestnut tree, interpreting the way the twigs had fallen, then noting a passing magpie. Satisfied with the signs, he walked on. The track, leading him into a small clearing, swung around to his right, where the forest's thicker canopy resumed.

The youth with the long mop of dark brown hair remained motionless, his eyes regarding the bedraggled figure as it came into his view. The sun broke cover from the thinning cloud to cast its brilliance into the small clearing, illuminating the vapour that arose from Jimmy's damp shoulders and creating more tiny rainbows that played about his head.

The young man was perched on the thick lower branch of a broad oak set back a little from the track, munching on a carrot. He kept his attention on Jimmy and wondered what riches his bag might contain. It certainly appeared to be a weighty burden, he thought to himself. As Jimmy reached the point where the track would lead him near to where it turned sharply to the right, he stopped and carefully laid his sack on the ground, flopping himself down next to it.

The glade echoed with birdsong and the play of a

hundred varieties of feathered creatures. Three young red squirrels caused a commotion across the clearing from him and suddenly darted by along the track. The young man watching from the tree could see them too, but he was careful to keep his gaze fixed on the youth with the bag of treasure, whom he was still just able to make out from his vantage point. Swathed in his long brown cloak, his eyes unblinking, the figure bit into another carrot and regarded the figure, who still appeared to be sitting at the edge of the glade.

Jimmy dragged himself back to his feet, made a great show of lifting the bag onto his shoulder and half-stumbled to where the squirrels still played at the bend in the track ahead of him, their stop-motion movements further complicated by the thin rays of sunlight that pierced the shadows, to endow little heads and bushy tails with momentary flecks of glory.

As he drew level with the oak, Jimmy stumbled again. Two of the squirrels vanished into the undergrowth. The other remained on the track, staring up at Jimmy from a shifting pool of sunlight. He looked down into the braver squirrel's face and winked conspiratorially.

"Ho there, fellow!" called the figure from the tree. As if struck by lightning, Jimmy fell to his knees, clutching the bag to his chest.

The young man, keeping his eyes on Jimmy all the

while, slipped down from the branch and was on the track in an instant, reaching for the knife at his belt. That was when he realized that, apart from the baffled squirrel, the track was deserted. He froze as something cold and clammy was held to his throat from behind him.

"Looking for this?" said Jimmy. He took the half-eaten carrot from the young man's neck to hold it up close to his face. The youth recognized the carrot as one he'd discarded just minutes before. His hands continued to search for his knife, but the sheath was empty.

"Or maybe this?" Jimmy moved around to stand in front of him, the carrot still held in front of the youth's face. Jimmy palmed the carrot so that the end protruded from between his curled forefinger and thumb. The youth narrowed his eyes, his jaw dropping when he saw that the end of the carrot was actually the handle of his own knife.

The squirrel, still only a few feet away from Jimmy and the youth, watched the piece of carrot as it fell onto the ground next to him. After a pause of less than a second, the squirrel left it where it lay and fled into the trees. Until now he had thought humans were a slow and plodding species. He would be much more wary of them in the future, he decided, wondering where his playmates might be.

Jimmy lowered his unclenched and empty hand, affording the youth a glimpse of his eyes. Disconcerted by what he saw there and infuriated at being outwitted, the youth lashed out with his fist. Stepping lightly back, Jimmy avoided the blow and moved to one side as the youth trod on the carrot and fell heavily onto his rear.

Then Jimmy froze. A dangerous-looking selection of blades were suddenly at his neck. Laughter from a score of throats rang through the trees as Jimmy was surrounded by a host of swarthy, armed men. The youth picked himself up from the ground and grabbed the front of Jimmy's damp smock.

"Where's my knife, you thief?"

Jimmy, unable to move for fear of decapitating himself, stared pointedly down at the youth's belt. Keeping his eyes on Jimmy, the youth reached down to grasp it, only to find that a small leather safety loop prevented it from being unsheathed. Grunting with anger and frustration, he danced off to his left, where he continued to attempt to wrestle the knife from its sheath. Jimmy watched as another figure appeared, back near the small clearing.

Jimmy's eyesight was second to none, but he *knew* that all there was first was a smile, walking towards him. Then, as if appearing from behind an invisible curtain, the rest of the body was suddenly standing two yards away, regarding him jovially from the centre of the track with its arms folded. Jimmy grinned up at the tall, bearded man, delighted with the trick. The youth had finally freed his knife and was marching towards Jimmy with it, but the mysterious newcomer snatched his arm and shook the weapon from his hand.

"Is that a fine way to treat a visitor to Sherwood, Will?" he said. The youth stalked away to sulk beneath the oak, his knife now back in its sheath. The tall man, whose hair was similar to that of the sullen youth, looked down into Jimmy's face, momentarily caught off balance as he tried to equate the ancient depths of his eyes with his apparent youthfulness. Jimmy, trying to keep his gaze averted, saw him gesture to the men who still held the knives at his throat. The blades were removed as one as the man stood back, smiling and holding his hand out to Jimmy.

"I am called Robin Hood around here. What is your name, lad?" The last word had been a question in itself.

"I am called James, sir, of York." They shook hands while Jimmy dodged Robin's searching glances. Robin let go of his hand and folded his arms, his look of amusement tainted slightly by intrigue.

"And what does James-sir-of-York have in his bag, pray?"

Will, the victim of Jimmy's sleight-of-hand, looked over, still scowling.

"Looked heavy when he was carrying it, Robin. Reckon it's silver – or maybe even gold?"

Jimmy walked to the other side of the track, reached into a tangle of undergrowth and, with a show of extreme effort, tugged the sack free of the brambles and dragged it across the ground to Robin. Jimmy puffed out his cheeks, put the palm of his hand into the small of his back and staggered away. Many of the other men were grinning at him knowingly. Everyone seemed to be enjoying themselves except Will, who now stared anxiously as Robin picked the sodden sack up from the ground.

Pausing to peer into its stuffy interior, Robin produced the ball with a flourish. He squeezed at the inflated pig's bladder and threw it to Will who, without time to calculate a response, took it on his right instep and swerved a nice pass to Jimmy, who caught it in his hands at waist level.

Robin was holding the sack upside down and shaking it to convince Will that he had once again been duped when a small, square piece of white paper fluttered out to land on the ground. Will walked quickly over and picked it up, tucking it slyly into a small bag that hung from his belt. Robin threw the sack to Jimmy and walked over to him.

"A child's toy, mayhap?"

Jimmy smiled, nodded, then shook his head as he put the ball back into the sack.

"Is it *magic?*" Robin tried to apply some sarcasm to the remark, but Jimmy had an answer for him.

"Yes, it is a child's toy, yes, it is a man's toy and *yes, it is magic!*" Jimmy had been very matter-of-fact in his reply until the last part, when he aimed a cautious look at Robin as he spoke.

"It's a football, Robin" he added as he swung the sack over his shoulder and prepared to continue along the track. Will and the others were vanishing back into the trees, while Robin walked alongside Jimmy around the bend in the track. Jimmy heard several of the men laugh in unison and caught a rustle of undergrowth from his left.

"So where do you aim for, young James?"

Jimmy tried to think of the name of a settlement south of there, but couldn't. "Erm..."

Robin laughed at Jimmy's response.

"Erm.. that's over in Dutchland somewhere, is it not? You're a long way off course, James of York!" They stopped walking and exchanged guarded glances for a while. There was more laughter and then someone called out, "Yoho! A tumble!"

Robin moved through the tangle of bushes as though they did not really exist, Jimmy following close behind. They came upon Will, rolling around and trading punches with another of the men. They broke from each other briefly as Robin stepped between them, his arms wide in a placatory gesture. "Enough!"

Both men were poised to spring at one another, but it was Will's face that burned the reddest. Robin waited between them until they had both calmed a little. He looked at Will's opponent, his expression serious as he did so. "What is all this about, Edric?"

Will tried to say something, but Robin silenced him with a glance. Edric, only seventeen years old himself, was trying hard not to laugh.

"I called him Will Scarlet, Robin" he managed eventually, after some sniggering.

Robin turned to Will and gravely regarded his bright red cheeks.

"He called me Will Scarlet, Robin!" he stated, rather needlessly.

Robin looked at Will, his expression immobile, then raised his eyebrows.

"So you would prefer to be known as Colin the Carrot, methinks?"

More laughter filtered through the trees around them as Robin turned to address the men. "A very special Lady Day feast tonight, my lads! Will Scarlet shall be celebrating his new name, and James of York shall be our *honoured* –" (Robin looked poignantly at Will as he stressed the word) "guest!"

Chapter 13

During the long centuries spent roaming the world, Jimmy had seen and even met some of the most powerful men on the planet; emperors, kings, warlords and chieftains. Almost without exception, all had bedecked themselves in expensive and garish adornments, ostentatiously bullying their way to, usually, a nasty, messy and early death. Jimmy had also seen some of the most beautiful women in history; Cleopatra; the Queen of Sheba; even once catching a glimpse of Helen of Troy getting out of the bath (one of Jimmy's favourite memories). But none of them were half so fair as the Lady Marian, he decided as he took a mouthful of fresh white crusty bread and tried to stop himself from staring at her again.

The young woman with the long, rich cascades of dark, chestnut-brown hair leaned sideways across Robin as he lay supported on an elbow beside her, next to a fire that blazed some ten yards from where Jimmy was sitting. She laughed prettily and sipped occasionally from a small pewter tankard, while Robin beamed at her, entranced by her every movement and spoken word. Jimmy sat by a smaller fire that crackled and spat near the edge of a large, elliptical clearing. Robin and a few of the others had sat with him at first, but when Robin had excused himself to be with his beloved, the others had drifted over to another fire nearby, leaving Jimmy alone to gnaw on the venison and sip the sweet-tasting mead from the horn he had been given on his arrival.

As the afternoon wore on, the shadows lengthened until the clear skies burned with gold. Jimmy cast his gaze across the scene. Maybe as many as a hundred and fifty men and women lounged, ate, drank and sported across the large glade. Smaller children ran around and played excitedly, while the older children served the others with food and drink, carefully picking their way back and forth between the needy revellers with jugs, baskets and gourds.

Jimmy caught himself staring at Marian again. She was looking back at him, her stern look only succeeding in making her look even more beautiful. He remembered what he'd been doing up to the point at which he'd become distracted, and was now picturing rustic goalposts at each end of the glade. The giant fellow, who was now sitting a few yards from him, eating and drinking as though it were a contest, was imagined in the goal to Jimmy's right, narrowing the angles against an onrushing striker. The image was confused by the deer and the hog that turned over the fires where the penalty spot would be, and by the accumulative effects of the mead.

Jimmy's silent reverie was broken by Robin's voice from his left.

"My Lady Marian pleases your eye, James of York, does she not?"

Jimmy blushed, but smiled his reply. "In truth Robin, I have never seen a more beautiful woman. I apologize for mine eyes, but they are their own men in this matter. I have no control."

Robin laughed and patted Jimmy's shoulder. "God's wounds, but that's a very good answer!" He leaned closer and added: "Especially from one of such tender years? You're a little older than you seem, James of York?"

Jimmy regarded the handsome figure of the leader of these men and tried to find some part of him that could be deemed 'ostentatious'. Then he tried to find some garish ornamentation that might set him apart from his fellows. Nothing. Were it not for his natural capability for leadership, this man would seem no different from the rest of the men who made so merry this day.

"Yes," said Jimmy, surprising himself. "I'm older than I

look." Jimmy hoped that Robin would leave the subject alone. He had never made such an admission to anyone before, though he had come close on several occasions.

He risked a quick look at Robin and saw that he was looking fondly over at Marian, who was now in conversation with the wives of some of the other men, laughing and jesting around another fire.

The giant fellow, having eaten to satiation and full of mead and wine, sank slowly backwards and gave vent to a loud and lengthy belch as his huge, shaggy head came to rest on the ground behind him. Jimmy watched a big, round man in a priest's robe career dangerously through the groups of people, clutching an empty tankard and earnestly searching for a refill. He was somehow maintaining an aura of someone holy and composed.

Robin's eyes took on a glassy sheen as he watched Marian accepting an apple from the basket of a little girl, resplendent, like the other children, in a headdress of wild flowers that hung down to frame her hair. Marian appeared to be telling the girl that she was the fairest maid in all the forest. Sure enough, the little girl's face lit up into a huge smile. Robin shifted his position as something stirred, deep in his soul.

"It was just over a year ago now," Robin began, his eyes still trained on Marian. "The Sheriff had proclaimed an archery contest between all-comers, to take place on the lawn within the castle walls. A bag of gold pieces to the best man with a longbow." Robin glanced briefly at Jimmy before returning his gaze to Marian.

"Knowing it to be naught but a trap for me, I forbade any of the others from attending, though most of them seemed to be there on the day."

A flight of wild geese passing by high overhead added to the general clamour in the clearing. A group of the smaller children were now clambering over the inert and snoring form of the sleeping giant. A little boy stood on the crest of his stomach and caused him to belch loudly, which dislodged three of the youngsters from his chest. Undaunted, they picked themselves up to begin climbing him again.

"So, disguised as an old tinker, I entered into the castle with everyone else on the day." Robin took a sip from his drinking horn and directed a broad grin at him, before once more seeming to become lost in his thoughts as he gazed once more at the beautiful woman. Jimmy drank from his mead horn and realized that he had emptied it more times than he could properly remember. The sky hung over his head like a big warm blanket. The pause lengthened until Jimmy was sure that Robin had forgotten he had been relating a tale.

"What happened?" said Jimmy, who was beginning to feel the effect of the mead. Robin looked back at him and grinned sheepishly.

"Oh, I won the contest," he said, somewhat offhandedly. "But the fun started when I went up to receive my prize from the Sheriff himself. No sooner had I gratefully accepted the handsome bag of money, than some fool in the crowd shouts out that I'm Robin Hood!" Robin sprang into a crouched position in front of Jimmy, his face a mask of mock terror.

"I slipped into a kitchen doorway and ran through a maze of fine corridors and landings; an hundred blades in hot pursuit! Until, by happy chance, I sought refuge through a door to a room up near the battlements." Robin's voice tailed off again as he re-lived the moment, the glassy sheen on his eyes more evident now. He sighed.

"And there she was! The lovely Maid Marian." Jimmy smiled with him as he tried to picture their first meeting. Robin sat back next to Jimmy as some young boys came by to add more wood to the fire.

Jimmy could see other children tending to the fires that burned throughout the glade. The large man in the priest's robe was coming towards where Jimmy and Robin sat, swaying from side to side like a ship on a stormy sea.

"She hid me in a linen chest and lied to the soldiers when they came to the room!" Robin went on. "When they had gone, I tripped getting out of the chest and dropped my bag of prize money, and the gold pieces scattered to the four corners of her room. Bless her heart!

She started to pick up the money but I bade her keep it. I told her that she was like a morning in May. Ha!"

Jimmy watched Robin choke back his emotions before continuing.

"I had fallen in love with her, do you see, James?" Jimmy smiled and nodded, then looked across to the drunken and huge holy man as he sank to the ground across the fire from them. Jimmy watched as he held his large tankard to his greasy jaws and tilt it to his lips, the wine streaming across his cheeks and jowls. His eyes half-closed, the holy man fished a dripping crude wooden crucifix from the cup, licked it clean and then dropped it so that it hung from his neck on its long, leather thong.

"A few days after that, Marian came to look for me in the forest. Thankfully, Little John found her before the Sheriff's men did and brought her to me. She had brought my prize money with her – every piece, love her!" Robin grinned at the big round man across from him. "Just a week after the contest, we were married right here by our solemn and dignified Friar Tuck."

While Robin had been speaking, the holy man had been trying to catch the eye of a young girl who had brought wine for the group of people behind him. His thick fingers holding out the empty tankard above and behind him, the Friar toppled backwards as the girl poured him more wine. Jimmy pushed Robin away to his left and then dived to his right as Friar Tuck's legs went up in the air.

It began like a swarm of angry bees, then quickly evolved into a gigantic, roaring ball of flame as the rush of gas from the Friar ignited in the flames of the fire. Jimmy looked over at Robin, the air between them full of freshly-agitated embers. Friar Tuck was back upright, quaffing happily from his tankard and seemingly unaware of the explosion. Jimmy noted that the Friar had taken the last of the wine from that particular jug, leaving none for the party that thirsted behind him. Jimmy smiled as he watched the girl indicate the Friar to the others as the reason for the lack of wine. She walked off to find more while one of the group tossed an apple at the holy man, bouncing it off his shoulder.

"Here, you greedy swine! You might as well have the last of our food while you're about it!"

The Friar looked down and saw the apple as if noticing it for the first time. He picked it up and sank his teeth into it, removing a quarter of it with one enormous bite and munching on it contentedly.

The sky had darkened further as evening approached. The children who had been clambering over the sleeping giant were now returned to their mothers, apart from three, who lay in various attitudes of sleep across the huge body. Two of the women from Marian's group were gathering them up from his chest and abdomen, to carry them off to their beds. A third woman searched for her infant, stumbling over the giant man's outstretched legs in her worry.

Stirred from his slumber by the woman's inadvertent contact, the giant sat up and, frowning thoughtfully, plucked the missing infant from beneath his vast beard, where it had been tucked between his neck and shoulder, sound asleep. The two-year-old girl curled up, still sleeping in the huge palm of his left hand. Jimmy watched the giant gently hold her out to her relieved mother as he rubbed at his face with his right hand.

Watching him closely all the while, Jimmy found the giant's face to be strikingly familiar, though they had never met before. It was when the huge man, stood up like a massive oak being felled in reverse, that Jimmy made the connection. He had seen likenesses in many churches in his travels and had heard tales of him. Could this be the Green Man in person?

Clad in a thick cloak of dark green, like so much foliage, the giant walked over to Robin, smiling broadly, though a little blearily.

"A great day, Robin! I'd better go and relieve Edric or he'll think I've forgotten him!" Little John's voice seemed to reach Jimmy's ears by way of a deep bass note via the ground.

"Good man, Little John! Shall we see you for the games on the morrow?" asked Robin.

Little John grinned back at him. "I wouldn't miss it for the world, Robin!"

Jimmy watched him walk away, noticing that the man's huge bulk seemed to disappear long before he'd reached the far side of the clearing. He turned to Robin and spoke before he could stop himself.

"Is Little John the Green Man, Robin?" said Jimmy with a frown. Robin got back to his feet again. After a longing glance at Marian, he turned to look at Jimmy, his eyes half-closed in a look of serious contemplation.

"A good question – and one I have oft considered myself."

Jimmy glanced up at him as Robin, his expression still set, moved his eyebrows and waggled them up and down comically.

"Methinks 'tis all the cabbage that he eats!" Robin crossed his eyes and grimaced. Jimmy laughed.

Robin was back with Marian again. Friar Tuck, who was still sitting upright across from Jimmy, seemed to be asleep. His eyes were closed and his messy jowls quivered with every loud snore. Jimmy realised that the Friar appeared to be snoring from both ends.

Jimmy was glad when Robin returned after a few minutes and suggested that he join him for his turn at the watch. As they made ready to go, Jimmy pointed at the Friar's sleeping bulk.

"What about Friar Tuck, Robin? Will he be all right?"

They looked down at him for a moment, stepping back when the noise from under his habit rose threateningly in pitch and volume. Robin smiled, pointing mysteriously at the sky.

"Don't worry about our friend the Friar. He is well looked after." Robin blew a kiss to Marian and led Jimmy into the darkening forest.

Chapter 14

Robin and Jimmy walked lightly through the gloom of the trees. Neither spoke as they approached the place where Will Scarlet sat in the leafy folds of a horse chestnut. Though still somewhat inebriated, Jimmy spotted the figure from a few hundred yards away, recognizing the shape of the young man he had outwitted earlier motionless on the lowest bough.

On reaching the base of the tree, they stopped. Jimmy looked down into a shallow valley, where a babbling stream ran from a dense area of woodland to his right along the floor of the valley that continued to his left. A rough track followed the stream, sandwiched between where Robin and Jimmy now stood and another thick expanse of forest on the far side.

Will dropped from his perch, landing the other side of Robin from Jimmy.

"Go and get yourself meat and drink, Will" said Robin. The young man nodded impassively at Robin's words, glaring dangerously at Jimmy all the while. Robin glanced back at Jimmy, who had just extended his right hand in Will's direction. Robin stepped back to lean against the tree, leaving Will to confront Jimmy's gesture of peace. Jimmy could see that Will's expression had not changed.

Will grinned slyly at Jimmy before aiming a more genuine smile towards Robin. Still with his eyes on his leader, Will held his right hand out towards Jimmy. With cat-like speed, Will grabbed Jimmy's forearm, wrestling him to the floor. Jimmy, however, had spotted the subterfuge, side-stepped, and was now looking down at the young man on the ground below him.

Will howled miserably as he realized that what had been Jimmy's forearm was actually just another half-eaten carrot. Deprived of his revenge, he hurled the vegetable into the ground, where it sprang back into the air to whirl down towards a tree by the side of the track in the valley below.

A squirrel, spending an evening of broken sleep in its snug little tree-hole, had been having bad dreams about humans who could chase and catch you, because they could suddenly move really fast. When the carrot came rattling in through the entrance to land with one end of it lodged against the inside of the tree and the other resting on the squirrel's left ear, it awoke in fear, not daring to move.

Will leapt to his feet and made to launch himself again at Jimmy. Robin took a step forward, but stopped when he noticed that Jimmy was holding out his hand again. It was holding a drinking horn. Jimmy raised it to his lips, took a sip and held it towards Will, who was again caught off guard.

Will carefully took the horn from Jimmy's hand, sniffed at it suspiciously and drank a mouthful of the sweet and heady mead. Robin stood between them again, but Will's fire was dying out.

Robin and Jimmy watched Will go back the way they had just come. Robin scaled the horse chestnut and was soon on the bough where Will had been perched. Jimmy found a comfortable place on a neighbouring branch. For a while they sat there and watched the sky become a deeper, darker blue; birdsong was still in evidence everywhere.

The silhouette of Robin's arm pointed down into the valley and Jimmy looked down to his right, where the stream burst from the thick undergrowth. A thick felled tree bridged across the water at this point, where the track came to an apparent end. Jimmy's gaze took in the winding gap in the canopy on the far side of the valley and deduced that the fallen tree was a crude crossing for the benefit of travellers using the track. Just to the right of the bridge Jimmy also noticed a tiny, foraging field mouse near a bush.

"See yon bridge?"

Jimmy nodded.

"Near where the field mouse is about to become a fox's supper?" Robin laughed quietly and shook his head. "My money is on Alan-a-Dale's mangy old tom cat."

Jimmy looked again and could just about see the black, shadowy shape, readying itself to pounce from near the fallen tree. The fox that Jimmy had spotted lurking in the bush was also on the verge of making its move.

A split second before the cat and the fox broke cover, the field mouse, perhaps sensing danger, stopped foraging, raised its tiny head and darted along the track.

Converging from opposite directions, the cat and the fox sprang at the mouse, but at the last instant, an owl swooped down to snatch the prize, leaving the furry hunters to share a brief accidental embrace before racing off into separate parts of the woodland. The owl alighted on the branch of a tree just down the slope from where Robin and Jimmy watched.

The owl, settling itself for its meal, was unaware of the carrot being pushed out of the hole in the tree above. The carrot landed on the owl's head, causing it to loosen its grip on the mouse, which ran down the tree and into a convenient hole. The owl hooted and flew off indignantly. Jimmy was just able to see the minuscule face of a terror-stricken squirrel peering cautiously out of the hole from where it had just ejected the carrot.

Robin's arm was almost completely concealed in the

deepening dusk as he pointed again to the makeshift bridge.

"That's where I first met Little John, on that bridge" he said. "He'd been fleeing a body of the King's men, having already laid low several of them, when I chanced to see him." Jimmy could see the grin animating his features, even in the gloom.

"If I had thought to ask him his business in the first place, I would have saved us both considerable time and effort. Being a younger and more headstrong Robin Hood, I leaped up onto the bridge and confronted him. I do remember that he looked tired and travel-weary, thinking that would be to my advantage. Ha!" He shook his head and chuckled quietly.

Jimmy looked down into the valley and noticed that an almost full moon had risen and was dusting the scene with silver.

"I brandished my stout oak staff at him and bade him come at me. Before I knew what had happened, I was face down in the stream with a sore head!" Robin laughed at the recollection, his eyes constantly checking his surroundings, even in his reverie.

Jimmy looked back from the bridge and was about to ask him what came next when Robin continued: "He picked me out of the water - with one hand, mark you - and put me on the bank as though I were no more than so much damp kindling. Then he stood over me and ordered me to take him to see Robin Hood!" He laughed again at the memory. "When I told him that it was *I* whom he sought, he wouldn't believe me. He said he'd heard that Robin Hood was twelve feet tall and the strongest man in all England!

"I had to take him to see the others to convince him, though I could see that he was not a little disappointed with me at first. John and his family were tired of constantly being overtaxed and harassed by the king's men and had heard the tales of some outlaws who had taken up residence in the forest of Sherwood."

Though Jimmy had been watching Robin as he spoke, he had not seen him move an inch, yet he was suddenly not there any more. He had vanished into thin air, just as he had first appeared to Jimmy after his encounter with Will. Jimmy glanced down at the stream in time to see a shadow fly across it and disappear into the woods beyond.

His keen eyes all around him, Jimmy peered into the gloom for any sign of Robin. The night air was warm and still; there was no sound or anything to see, and yet he was back in his original position on the branch. Jimmy leaped to his feet, completely confused. Robin looked up at him and casually raised his hand reassuringly.

"Twas only old Olaf, the poacher. He lives not far from here. He's bagged a brace of..."

"How do you *do* that, Robin?" Jimmy was agitated, not being used to seeing real magic performed. He had witnessed many conjurors and had, up until now, been able to explain away the subterfuge. "Was the mead I drank so strong or are you faster than the eye can see?"

Robin's smile was mysterious. "Methinks we are each a puzzle to the other" he said

Neither spoke for several minutes, each considering the other within the foliage as the moonlight cast mercurial pools of lace around them. Jimmy was making up his mind to tell Robin about his extraordinarily long past, but couldn't think where to start. He glanced at Robin, who still kept a constant watch on their surroundings, and wondered how this enigmatic figure was able to appear and disappear at will. It was then that Jimmy recalled a long distant memory.

The recollection was hazy and indistinct from spending over two thousand years near the bottom of Jimmy's crowded mind, but more came back to him as he continued his silent contemplation. Even back then he had been a considerable age, though his physical appearance would be identical with the way he looked here, in the early thirteenth century AD.

He had been travelling in the land of the ancient Etruscans and had spotted a crowd of workmen at a place they called Tarquinii, digging foundations for a temple.

Concealing himself nearby, Jimmy had noticed an approaching thunderstorm, building up a giant black anvil of towering cloud to the south of the excavations. Hidden in some trees to the north of them, he waited for the weather to hand him his cue.

A blinding flash of lightning had been followed closely by a colossal clap of thunder, and Jimmy had made his move. When the men had looked back to where they had been digging, Jimmy had appeared to them to spring from the ground. By pure chance, Jimmy's cause had been helped further when several of the startled diggers had made to grab him. Jimmy had merely raised his hands defensively, but another nearby lightning strike and peal of thunder had transformed the gesture into something much more impressive.

They had led him from the site and taken him to their elders, who named him Tages. But it had all happened so very many years ago.

Jimmy remembered being surprised at the time that no one had seemed capable of foretelling events with any degree of accuracy. Over the centuries, he had taught himself the art of xylomancy and many other forms of fortune-telling, having already studied the subject at school in his youth (the people from the ancient part of the planet he had come from had been developing the science for quite some time). Somewhat condescendingly, Jimmy had spent a few years writing the Acherontian books, explaining patiently to the ancient people all the different ways of predicting the future, from the date and location of the birth of the new Messiah, to 'is my husband/wife being faithful?' Tages finished the books, left them in possession of the most trustworthy person in Tarquinii and continued his travels when his inability to age physically began raising the inevitable embarrassing questions.

Jimmy watched the field mouse re-emerge from its hiding place and make its way back to where it had been foraging earlier, while he considered the amount of influence his books had had. The original scrolls would have long since perished of course, but much of it had been preserved and handed down, still practised through the long centuries, disseminated by the various doctrines who utilised at least parts of this knowledge. It seemed likely to Jimmy that the people of this mediaeval world knew plenty about such things. All the same, he was disappointed with himself for not having anticipated the outcome of the field mouse incident – nor Robin's incredible disappearance. Some of the basic fundamentals of his impressive knowledge of life's lesser-known machinations were being called into question in this curiously vibrant forest. He decided to tell Robin more about himself the next evening over another taste of the delicious and heady mead, little realizing that the moment had passed.

Chapter 15

The following day, after another small feast and more of the excellent mead, the games began. Jimmy was extremely impressed by the feats of skill, dexterity and strength of many of Robin's band of outlaws throughout their various displays and contests, but he silently swore that sorcery was being employed when the archery competition got under way. Positioning himself as near to the tiny targets as he dared, Jimmy watched every arrow as it flew to the mark. The difference between each archer's score was microscopic, such was the standard. Robin took the prize, as he had done every year, handing the handsome and ancient drinking horn that was his annual trophy to the fair Maid Marian, their hug and kiss toasted and cheered by the crowd.

The prize, a two-thousand-year-old drinking vessel from Babylon, was wrapped with elegantly-wrought silver in the form of leafy vines which had survived well, considering its long and turbulent history. Jimmy watched as it was filled with mead and handed back to Robin.

"Long life, health and happiness to you all!" He took a swig from the ancient horn and handed it to Marian, who then passed it on.

"Now we are going to try out a new game that our young friend, James of York, shall now attempt to teach us." There were several voices raised questioningly, echoing Jimmy's own thoughts as he tried to recall even mentioning here anything about teaching anyone a new game. Jimmy looked up at Robin with his face a compendium of emotions and found himself getting to his feet.

Most of the younger and leaner men hovered around Jimmy in eager anticipation as they listened to his explanation of the rules, though several of the more mature members of this wooded commune had joined their ranks. Splitting them into two teams of - as it worked out - eleven, Jimmy supervised the building of the rustic goalposts he'd envisaged the previous day and placed the ball in the centre of the large clearing. The two appointed captains walked over to him while two other inflated pigs bladders were being kicked around by each team for a warm-up. Robin had not included himself among the players; he was languishing with his fair Lady Marian under the glorious canopy of a mighty oak on a naturally raised bank near the halfway line.

Jimmy looked up into the face of one of the captains.

"What is your name and from whence do you hail?"

The tall youth frowned slightly, brightened and replied: "I am Harold and I hail from Bridge Stowe." Jimmy had never heard of the place before.

"Is that near here?"

Harold smiled and shook his head. "No zur, it be down near Baff where the Abbey is."

Jimmy was impressed. This youth had some travelling under his belt. He turned and looked up into the face of Will Scarlet, the other captain. "And from where do you hail, Will?"

His arms folded and his weight on his left foot, Will casually raised an eyebrow and exuded arrogance.

"Me? I was born here, in the forest."

"Well that gives you home advantage!" Will frowned as he considered Jimmy's remark. They turned to regard Robin and Marian and Jimmy paused to allow the cheers and applause to abate. He took a deep breath.

"My lords and ladies! For your amusement and pleasure I give you a contest of skill and strength. Football!" While allowing the cheers and whistling to again die down, Jimmy had a brainwave. "A contest between the Sherwood Foresters," he went on, indicating the sheepish Will Scarlet, "and the Bridge Stowe Rovers!"

Jimmy tossed the coin and Harold guessed correctly.

Will, while still exhibiting a façade of aloof unconcern, was nonetheless getting agitated. Harold kicked off and the Rovers launched into the first attack of the game. Jimmy, who had thought it best to referee the match, was astounded by how quickly everyone seemed to accustom themselves to it. There was laughter and catcalls from the players and from most of the crowd as the ball bounced around perilously near to the Foresters' goal. After a frantic goalmouth scramble, which left several of the players and most of the crowd in hysterics, the ball rebounded over to the left wing, where Harold outwitted a defender with the drop of a shoulder and fired the ball back with the outside of his left foot.

There was a hush as the ball looped over everyone's head and swerved past Little John's reach, hurtling into the top corner. One-nil to the Rovers!

The crowd cheered and Jimmy whistled to acknowledge the goal. Before anyone needed any more prompting from Jimmy, the ball was brought back to the centre and the Foresters, having seen the Rovers team demonstrate it, launched their first attack.

The ball came to Will near the edge of the Rovers penalty area and he shaped up for a long-range effort. It was at that moment that Jimmy noticed something else that struck him as extremely peculiar.

It seemed that a small child, clad in a wild array of

velvet rags in various shades of green and brown, had been patiently waiting for the ball to come to him. As Will swung his right foot to strike the ball, the child nudged it slightly, making Will slice his shot well wide of the goal. Jimmy put his fingers to his mouth to whistle, but decided against it when the child simply vanished into the ground. None of the players had noticed anything untoward or strange, not even Will, who turned away from his attempt with a look of self-disgust. While the ball was being retrieved for the goal kick to be taken, Jimmy wondered what this odd phenomenon could have been.

Though there had been numerous chances throughout the rest of the first half, the score remained at one-nil when Jimmy decided to call a halt for half-time. As the players staggered off the field to receive refreshment and a rest for their weary limbs, Robin and Marian came down from their 'executive box' to greet Jimmy.

"A wondrous exciting game, good James! There is more, I hope?" It was Marian who spoke and Jimmy, intoxicated by her sheer loveliness, flailed for an answer.

"We have played but half of it, be assured, my lady. I am overjoyed that it appeals to you." Jimmy was trying not to get drawn into her eyes and was relieved when Robin came to his rescue.

"James of York, methinks we'll play this again! Everybody is praising it! There is more, did you say?"

Marian excused herself to return to her seat and Jimmy took this advantage to ask Robin if he had noticed anything strange about Will Scarlet's first goal attempt. Robin smiled at him and dropped down on his haunches so that his mouth was close to Jimmy's ear.

"What did *you* see?" whispered Robin, keeping his features carefully configured. Jimmy quietly described what he had seen and glanced repeatedly at him for any signs of corroboration.

Robin looked at him and grinned. "It seems to me that you have seen Jack-in-the-Green at work. A mischievous imp! Fear not, James. He'll do no harm."

The second half saw the Foresters apply a long spell of early pressure on the Rovers' defence. Several times the ball rattled the goalposts as the Bridge Stowe team stood their ground. Will Scarlet was proving to be a worthy centre-forward, constantly wrong-footing the defenders and possessing a lethal strike from either side. A long-range effort from his right foot thudded into the middle of the top of the crossbar, snapping it in two. Play was held up while the Bridge Stowe goalkeeper repaired it with a slim branch and some cord.

Will took the opportunity to retrieve the small square of white paper from his pouch and look at it closely. Unable to read, he nonetheless knew what words and letters looked like. The characters were faded and barely discernible and many were not words or letters at all, he noticed. Much, the miller's son, came over to him. Secretively, Will turned away and slipped the paper back into his pouch, convinced that he was in possession of what could only be a magic spell.

Still watching keenly from the knoll, Robin was already adamant that the goalposts would have to be a much more robust structure for future games. He hugged Marian and momentarily distracted from the field of play, noticed how everyone seemed to be completely transfixed by the game. When Will's cannonball had broken the bar, a young and impressionable woman, watching from near the far corner flag, had collapsed in a faint. But what struck the outlaw leader most was the way everyone seemed to be chatting excitedly to one another, gesticulating as they tried to communicate to their fellows the wonders they had witnessed.

The game resumed, and the ball was punted high into the air. Jimmy watched it for a moment as it sailed through the sky. As he was about to run upfield to where a crowd of Foresters defenders vied with Harold and a few of the other Rovers forwards for the approaching ball, he stopped in his tracks. There she was!

An eternity of confused memories ran unchecked around Jimmy's brain as his eyes locked onto the figure of the girl, who was beckoning to him from the far end of the clearing. As though moving through deep water, he waded sluggishly towards the girl, who had now moved into the shade of the forest. Glancing at the twigs beneath the trees for some kind of hint of what might be happening, he could see only clusters of sinister question marks. He abandoned his accepted knowledge of the universe to the suddenly-tangible wind, while his body entered a different dimension.

Daunted also by an overwhelming certainty that he was in danger, he nonetheless strived to catch the girl. The football match was now of only secondary importance to him. The sound of the crowd and the players had vanished, replaced by an eerie melody that swooped and soared above the chaos in his head. Certain parts of the air unlocked different memories for him, when he had seen the girl with the terrifying eyes and the inescapable allure in the distant past. However often he recalled these memories, he was never able to remember actually catching up with the girl, nor, indeed, the outcome of the chase.

The urge to reach her drove him on regardless, the edge of the clearing becoming nearer all the time. The music he was hearing sounded like the soft yearnings of a young woman, though much of it put him in mind of a wooden flute. Despite feeling certain, within himself, that he would never catch up with the girl, Jimmy pushed himself hard, his eyes still firmly focused on the spot where he had seen her last.

Robin leaned forward as the goalkeeper prepared to take the goal kick. He watched Jimmy as he, in turn, watched the ball sail through the air. A small crowd of players ran between Robin and Jimmy. When they had passed, Jimmy was nowhere to be seen.

Robin was on the pitch and had whistled to halt the game before the ball had reached the crowd of players upfield. "Take the goal kick again! James of York has had to leave, so I shall referee the rest of the match!"

No one, except for Robin, had noticed Jimmy's sudden disappearance, but the game resumed nevertheless. The referee's sudden disappearance into thin air promised to be quite a talking point – except that it was completely eclipsed by what happened next.

William of Steepledon, the Bridge Stowe goalkeeper, decided to put more effort into the retaken goal-kick, connecting with the ball perfectly and with great force. The ball became a blur as it cleared the halfway line at shoulder-height and continued to rise while the players, aghast at the ferocity of the clearance, fought to get out of the way of its trajectory. Little John, who, as the Foresters' goalkeeper, had had little to do for the previous five minutes, was unsighted when the ball rocketed across the field. It was now dipping slightly, though it seemed destined to clear the top of his goal.

Robin knew, from the moment a blackbird broke cover from the trees, what the outcome would be, though he was as surprised as everyone else when it happened. Halfway across the glade, the bird exploded in a cloud of feathers as the ball thundered into it and it dropped towards the ground. Still travelling at considerable speed, the ball screamed straight down at Little John, who failed to sense the danger until it glanced off the back of his head, bounced off the ground, rebounded off the crossbar and arced over him.

He turned, fully expecting to find the ball in the net. As the dead blackbird dropped on his head, the ball, subject to a substantial amount of backspin, kicked into the ground behind him, dislodged the bird from his head and bounced into the goal. The giant threw back his vast, shaggy head and roared with laughter.

"Two nil!" Robin whistled, chuckling at the outrageous turn of events while still casting about him for any sign of James of York.

Chapter 16

Still forcing himself through air that had now taken on the consistency of dense treacle, Jimmy battled with foliage that seemed more and more entangled with every step. Then, stifling and void of energy, Jimmy felt himself begin to lose consciousness. He slumped as his body gave in, but then he jumped back upright. He found he was standing right next to the young girl, who was sitting on a huge mushroom, casually breaking off pieces of the fungus and eating them.

"Hello Tages. How are you, my dear?"

Jimmy's mind reeled – this girl was more familiar to him than anything in his life, but he couldn't think of her name. *Tages?* He hadn't been called that for well over a thousand years!

"I… know you, don't I?" His voice sounded faltering and sluggish in his own ears. The girl looked at him kindly, leaving her strange smile to explain everything, as though waiting for his memory to get up to speed. She held out a piece of the mushroom to him.

"Have some?" He frowned at the fungus and then at her. She shrugged when he failed to react to her offer, then ate the piece herself, regarding him with a calm good humour. The forest around them was still and perfectly quiet. He watched her consume the pieces of mushroom, fascinated by the way her rosebud mouth and cheeks remained motionless all the while beneath those eyes that mirrored his own perfectly.

It was at that moment that Jimmy felt an overwhelming urge to reveal to this girl how he really felt about her, before something else happened and the chance was lost. Scattered and tantalisingly vague memories were dashing past his mind's eye, little of which helped to resolve the issue of who or what this girl actually was. He did, however, have a strong feeling that she would be gone again soon.

"What is your name?" His voice no longer as hesitant as it had been before, but it nevertheless sounded slurred and foolish in his ears.

The girl flashed her eyes at him and opened her mouth. Jimmy concentrated hard, convinced that she would vanish before revealing her identity to him.

"Don't you remember me, Tages?" Her words were a

passage from some wonderful score for solo wooden flute. Jimmy continued to flounder as he tried to separate the words from the music and attempt to make some sense of them. He was still a long way off making a coherent reply when she supplied the *leitmotiv* of the most beautiful symphony he would ever hear in his long, long life.

"I am Lilith, your half-sister" she said.

They exchanged glances for a few moments as Jimmy fought to digest this information, though it was difficult to extricate it from the lovely tune. The images that flickered through his brain began to make a kind of sense, but it was all spread out over an incredibly long period of time, and the treacle he had fought through to get himself here seemed to have infiltrated his brain.

She offered him another piece of mushroom. This time he held his hand out to her, albeit in super-slow-motion. Fascinated by the pink flesh of the fungus, he regarded it for a moment before popping it into his mouth. Instantly, he felt the treacle in his head recede. He looked at her and smiled.

"I love you."

"I know you do, Tages. And I know that you always shall love me. Here, have some more of this and maybe you'll be able to work it out."

Her reply completely disarmed him. Feeling completely vulnerable, his heart seemed to break into a million tiny fragments when she laughed – though it was not an unkind laugh. Keeping his eyes on her tiny face, he took the second piece of fungus and put it into his mouth. His mind cleared, but he was still having trouble taking all this in.

"Then who were our parents, Lilith?" he asked. The girl rolled her eyes in such a way that it seemed the whole universe wheeled beneath her small brows, making Jimmy feel giddy and not a little queasy. Jimmy was trying desperately not to look too hard at her eyes, but he could not help himself. The forest, the mushroom and Lilith all disappeared as he tumbled into her hypnotic gaze. Unsure if it would have any effect, Jimmy closed his eyes against the chill, never-ending procession of stars and planets. Immediately he felt better, though his body now seemed cramped and uncomfortable. He felt warmer though; still alive, if his sore arm was anything to go by. He tried to speak, but he was now obviously within a very confined space.

"Lilith?"

The effort of speaking her name seemed to exhaust him completely and he dropped into a deep sleep, his dreams peopled with strange, distant memories and beautiful music set against a vast backdrop of gargantuan planets and impossibly old constellations. In his dream, Jimmy began searching for her, wandering a long and fruitless succession of barren, desolate and uninhabited worlds.

After an eternity of this, Jimmy was awoken by voices. The huge planet he had just trudged over was now forgotten as his eyes rolled slowly open. His left arm was very sore now, and he felt a little hungry. Bright sunlight made him blink, though all he was able to see was something that looked like wood, very close up. A few ants walked across his limited field of vision.

Jimmy worked his left arm from its cramped quarters, feeling the blood begin to flow through its veins again. He turned his head slightly to his left and began to realise where he now was; the sunlight was reaching him via a hole in the trunk of a tree.

By the time he had managed to free himself from the inside of the yew tree, the sound of the voices had gone. Lying on the soft undergrowth in the forest in the cool of a spring evening, Jimmy looked at the tree, wondering how long he had been in there and how he had come to be inside it in the first place. Reaching down into the narrow opening, he pulled the ancient sack from the hole in the tree; the pig's bladder within was still inflated. Still wearing his brown cloak, which seemed thinner and more faded, Jimmy rolled himself up in it and slept until the following morning, little realizing that he had been subject to an entirely accidental inter-dimensional shift which had deposited him almost six centuries into the future and a fair distance from Sherwood Forest.

One year after Jimmy's disappearance, the two teams were preparing for the second annual Sherwood Forest Cup football match. Robin walked over to Will. Since the day the stranger had vanished, Will had become much less fiery. When battling with the Sheriff's men, he was as tenacious and hot-blooded as ever, but now he moved and spoke with a kind of quiet grace, forever seeking the positive side of everything. The young maidens in the forest had unanimously made him their prime catch, and his brooding scowl had given way to a contented smile. He now insisted that he be called Will Scarlet and always spoke fondly of his memories of the boy from York who had bested him and shown him the error of his former ways. He was also the glade's top goal scorer.

"You won the archery contest this morning, Will. Why won't you admit it?" said Robin. Will flushed, trying not to notice the young women on the touchline all chanting his name. A ball came over to him near the halfway line and he casually volleyed it into the top corner of the distant goal, rocking the structure as it spun in the netting. Several of the girls swooned, while the others shrieked their approval. Red-faced, Will turned to regard his friend.

"No, Robin, yours was the closest arrow, I'm sure." His eyebrows raised and shaking his head, Robin caught his gaze and held it.

"I've known you since you were a tiny, tearaway villain,

Will. You have always tried to be the best at everything and, now you *are* the best, you try to deny it. Why, Will? What has happened to you? You seem so different."

The two teams were almost ready to start the game. Will, eventually drawing away his gaze from his leader, seemed to make his mind up. "I'll tell you at half-time Robin, I promise."

Will took up his position at the centre spot, while Robin, having taken it upon himself to be the referee again, took a quick look around the field and, satisfied that everyone was ready, whistled for the commencement of the match. He was startled by the effect it had had, because the cheer from the crowd was a mighty roar which only occasionally dimmed to an excited, almost electrical, hum.

As with the previous year's game, the pace was fast and furious. Everyone on both teams was playing exceptionally well, though the player who stood out, head and shoulders above the rest, was Will Scarlet. Every time the ball came anywhere near him, the volume of the crowd's cheering increased. Despite the circumstances, Will would always trick his opponent with a piece of devastating skill and find a distant colleague with an inch-perfect pass.

Several times, Robin quite clearly saw Jack-in-the-Green trip someone likely to dispossess Will, and also give the Sherwood Foresters the 'luck of the bounce' in a fifty-fifty situation, though the game was still goalless as half time approached. Despite being the centre-forward, Will could have scored any number of times, but was unselfishly trying to tee up his team mates to actually put the ball into the net.

The crowd, however, were becoming frustrated with his performance and wanted to see him have an attempt on goal himself, especially as his team-mates, while playing out of their skins, were all failing to find the net. Little John, sitting with his back against a goalpost down the other end and drinking from a horn of mead, joined the chorus from the crowd.

"Scar-*let!* Scar-*let!* Scar-*let!* Scar-*let!*"

As referee, Robin watched everything carefully. There had been no fouls and the game had been played in a good spirit by both teams. The goalkeeper ran up to take the goal kick, but as he did so his standing leg was pulled sideways by a small, almost imperceptible child in velvety green and brown. The kick was sliced, though it appeared to be travelling towards one of his own defenders. Will trotted a little closer to where the defender was, though he could see that there was no way he would reach the ball before him, so he was quite surprised when the defender fell over for no apparent reason. Instantly sprinting to the ball, Will glanced around for any signs of support, though it seemed that everyone else was still back down the other end of the field, awaiting the long goal kick clearance that never came.

The fallen defender was quickly back on his feet. With several other opponents nearby to close him down, Will swung his right foot back and shot first time, albeit from an extremely acute angle.

Everyone in the glade held their breath as the ball left the front instep of Will's foot to soar over the heads of the defenders and the stranded goalkeeper. When it went in off the top of the far post the entire glade erupted. Will was carried back to the centre line by his team mates and it took several minutes to clear the ecstatic young women from the pitch before the game could be restarted.

Despite there being only two more minutes of the half left to play, Will came off the field with a hat-trick, a broad grin dividing his face as he walked over to Robin for a well-earned drink. Robin laughed as he ushered the crowd of young women away.

"You can have him *after* the game, ladies!" He turned to Will and his expression became more serious for a moment.

"So, Will. Tell me why you have changed so much. What's the secret?"

Will's smile turned to a knowing grin. From a pouch on his belt he tenderly drew a small bag and holding it close to his chest, he pointed at it with his other hand.

"It's a magic spell, Robin! I – I – I found it!"

Robin raised an eyebrow and gave him a searching

look. Will, almost lapsing automatically into the sulk of his old self, quickly checked himself and came clean.

"I *did* find it. It fell out of James's bag last year, when you turned it upside down."

Robin nodded, recalling the event in his mind, and held his hand out. Although, of all the people in the world, he knew Robin was the most trustworthy of them all, Will was still reluctant to hand him the bag, scared, possibly, that the spell would be broken and his new-found good fortune lost forever.

After the briefest of pauses, Will put the bag in his hand and watched closely as Robin carefully took the small, rolled-up piece of paper from within. Being about as literate as Will, Robin read out the letters slowly, while Will sipped nervously from his mead and glanced about him for any signs that his luck was ending.

"S - a - i - n - s - b - u - r - y's - m - a - k - i - n - g - l - i - f - e - t - a - s - t - e - b - e - t - t - e - r" read Robin. He too felt that the paper, so very thin and faded, was truly ancient and magical. There were more letters below, followed by strange symbols he had never seen before.

"S - t - e - e - p - l - e - d - o - n... these words mean nothing to me. Mayhap we should consult the Friar? He is a man of learning and a cleric."

Will's flashing smile had gone out, but he pointed to the bottom of the paper at a word he recognised, next to more of the unknown symbols.

"*Change,* Robin! That word says *change!* Don't you see? Thanks to James of York and his magic spell, I have *changed!*" Robin watched the smile creep back across Will's face and scrutinized the six-letter word on the spell before rolling it back up and replacing it in the small bag. As he handed Will back the bag, he knew that James of York had only been the catalyst and the spell only a 'magic feather'. Will's transformation had come from within himself, of this he was certain.

Eager now to get on with the match to see if the spell still worked, Will finished his mead, tossed the empty tankard to the scores of raised arms from a cluster of female admirers – all fighting to claim it – and, blowing them a kiss, ran onto the pitch. Robin grinned broadly at the frenzied young women, then felt a hand on his shoulder. He turned and felt his heart miss a beat as Marian, lovelier than ever, looked deep into his eyes, holding him spellbound.

"Don't ever change, my love," she said.

Chapter 17

The two brothers sullenly moved towards the front door, their irate father having handed out yet another scolding for their misbehaviour. They had been banished to the forest for the afternoon; to collect firewood ostensibly, but the main motive had been to get them out of the house, where they had been kicking a pair of rolled-up socks around until it had upset their mother and, ultimately, their father. Their slow and deliberate gait had suddenly become a mad dash across the meadows as their sense of fun once again held sway.

Reaching the edge of the forest, the two boys quickly amassed two large piles of firewood and kindling, which they lashed into two huge bundles, ready to take home with them. Taller by an inch and a half and older by just over a year, Percy sprinted into the trees, returning shortly with a round, inflated pig's bladder. His brother Tristram shouted excitedly as his brother ran towards him, the ball bobbling over the uneven ground as he dribbled it towards him.

"Where did you get *that,* Perce?" Tristram ran to him and tackled him expertly, leaving his brother off-balance and wrong-footed. Percy chased him back towards the trees, determined to reclaim it. Tristram stopped and flicked the ball up to catch it in his hands when a strange boy appeared from his left and intercepted the ball with a scrawny knee. The two brothers stopped as Jimmy ran towards the younger of them, dodging and weaving with the ball near his feet, but never quite where it ought to have been. Jimmy spent a few minutes running rings around them until Percy suddenly got his foot to the ball, directing it towards his brother, who likewise became suddenly galvanized. It was nearly dark by the time the boys staggered home with their large bundles of wood.

During the day, another ten youngsters from the nearby village of Steepledon had happened along, joining in the fun. Jimmy got them all to promise to return the next day, then walked back to the trees. He sniffed the evening air and spent an enjoyable three hours reading what the apparently random falls of twigs were conveying to him. A little later the song of a lone nightingale filled in many of the gaps until, satisfied with his long study and ultimate interpretation, he dozed beneath the yew.

Chapter 18

It had all seemed straightforward enough to Wilf when he had signed up that day with his mate Eddie. Everyone else was doing the same and it was easy to get carried along. The way everyone spoke, it was just a matter of helping France and Belgium against the Kaiser and his lot. With any luck the whole thing would be done and dusted by Christmas and they'd all be back with their loved ones.

Wilf was eager to get back to playing football again; he kept expecting to find a group of his old friends from the days when they used to meet up near where they all lived, kicking a cabbage around a level area of Belgian soil. In retrospect it hadn't been that long ago when he would call around Eddie's house to go racing off to meet the others at the park, thumping the ball around until it was too dark to see it any more.

"D'you reckon the other boys from Steepledon are over here somewhere too, Eddie?" he asked.

They had been marching for much of the day and had called a halt at a place that was much closer to the German front line than intelligence had anticipated. They swigged hot sweet tea from their mess tins and shared a Woodbine. There was gunfire in the distance but there seemed to be no urgency among any of the officers he could see. Eddie scratched his left ear, thoughtfully, and continued to cast his gaze about him.

"I 'eard the 'ole lot of 'em's in different outfits – Roger Carlson's joined the navy" he said. "'E could be bleedn' anywhere now. Why? You wants a game a football, I spec.'"

The sound of gunfire was suddenly a lot closer and both soldiers tensed, ready to spring into action, though it appeared that they were the only ones there to be aware of any threat. Both Wilf and Eddie were wishing themselves back on home turf at that moment. It seemed the most wonderful place to be and the most wonderful thing to be doing; chasing a tatty old ball around the park – even during any of those days when it had rained, when they had all showed up and played anyway, despite the weather, *and* played better than ever. The faces of friends and the amusing moments during a game never to be forgotten were foremost on their minds.

The tea and the cigarette were finished absent-mindedly and they remained poised to jump to an order.

"Yer, Wilf, what happened to young Jimmy 'Awk?" The gunfire had become more sporadic. Nonetheless, both 17-year-olds remained alert. Wilf glanced at his friend and smiled.

"His name was Jimmy *York,* Eddie. Jimmy *York.* Why?"

Eddie's face took on a slightly stubborn expression as he glanced around him. "Well, *I* always called 'im Jimmy 'Awk, 'cause of 'is eyes. I never seen eyes like *they* before!" Wilf turned to focus his attention on his friend as a number of memories were stirred from their slumber in the sleep-deep chambers of his mind.

"I know what you mean! I always thought he was a strange 'un meself. I never found out where he lived – or even if he had any kin."

"And 'ow old *was* 'e, any'ow?" Wilf returned Eddie's quizzical stare. Jimmy had looked about ten years old when Wilf and Eddie first began playing football in the park. Both had been barely six years old at the time, and all the others were older then, though they had never felt intimidated as a result of their youth. There had been a space for two midfielders in the team and they had been accepted as though the rest of them had known them for much longer than their years would merit. And all the time the rest of the team grew older and physically bigger, Jimmy still looked like a ten-year-old kid.

"About ten?"

Eddie, still wrapped up in his reverie, missed his friend's reply. The gunfire was being punctuated by explosions. Wilf repeated his response. Eddie looked at him, his young face lined with puzzlement.

"He was a bloody good footballer, mind" stated Wilf. He remembered the only time he had ever managed to tackle Jimmy, and he had been so surprised that he'd lost the ball to someone else before he'd been able to do anything with this unexpected possession.

"I never saw *any*one play football like him" added Wilf, his attention now on a group of officers standing in a group thirty yards away. There was more shooting and then something was suddenly exploding from the chest of a soldier walking away from where they had been marching. The man fell forward and lay still on the ground. Transfixed by the sight of someone being killed, Wilf didn't hear his friend's reply. Eddie had been distracted by the sight of the town through a clump of trees, wondering what it might be called.

"I never seen anyone *move* like 'im. You'd as well catch a ghost."

"Eddie. That soldier – that man over there's just got shot in the back! I bloody saw it, Eddie!"

"Eh?"

When the officer came over to muster them for action, both men were dazed and took a moment to respond.

"Get yer arses up and ready to fight for your lives! We're being surrounded by the Hun and we've got to fall back – double bloody quick! Come *on!*"

Wilf and Eddie ran over to the dead soldier, lifting him by his lifeless shoulders and running with him after the rest of their fleeing comrades. One of the younger officers approached them and ordered them to leave the dead man, though his words were completely drowned by a prolonged burst of gunfire. Wilf and Eddie, still clinging to the dead soldier, burst into a sprint, sending the officer the wrong way with a beautifully-timed combined dummy.

"Ha ha…" Eddie's nervous laughter was cut short when he felt another bullet thud into the corpse they still sprinted with. When they caught up with the rest of their comrades they found themselves sheltering in a slight undulation in the middle of a field. The Germans were still encircling them and, with evening approaching, were gathering in numbers. As they laid their fallen comrade between them on the ground, they both wrinkled their noses and looked at one another.

"Smells like bonfire smoke" suggested Eddie.

Wilf nodded. "Yes, but it smells too sweet. What on earth is it?"

The air was turning a pale green and the smell was becoming overpowering, while the sun seemed to dim in the sky. The gunfire from the Germans had faltered and the scene was becoming eerily quiet. Wilf watched in wonder as an assortment of enemy shells fell in a neat line along the edge of the field. When another fusillade came out of the trees, Wilf saw the shells drop harmlessly among the others. Something was protecting them, he thought to himself, and said a quiet prayer of thanks.

General H.L. Smith-Dorrien regarded his men and turned to his officers.

"We've got to make a run for it before dark, chaps, or we'll all be slaughtered like dogs." Together, the General and his officers surveyed the route back to safety; gunfire and an occasional cannon shell were criss-crossing the way between the closing pincers of the enemy all around them. As they all looked back to give the order to run for their lives, Wilf and many of the others were suddenly on their feet and pointing in wonder.

The sounds of gunfire and roaring cannon were completely hushed as the air became filled with the strains of strangely beautiful music. Two long rows of men clad in faded green formed a narrow corridor that stretched beyond where the Germans were preparing to close the trap. Wilf and Eddie picked up the dead soldier and followed the others as they ran across the field.

The men lining the corridor were all equipped with longbows, and were loosing a steady stream of phosphorescent arrows toward the Germans on either side of them, their quivers bristling and behaving like large, spectral wings at their backs. Wilf and Eddie swore afterwards that they both saw faces they recognised among the ranks of the mysterious archers as they ran with their dead comrade to safety, though neither could put a name to any of them.

Eddie later found out that the town he had seen had been called Mons. The 3rd and 4th Divisions of the Old Contemptibles had escaped when a massacre had seemed the only possible outcome.

Chapter 19

From within the colossal natural boundaries of huge and impenetrable mountain ranges emerged a race of people in complete isolation from the rest of the world. In the year 5212 BC an asteroid had devastated huge tracts of land and effectively cut off large numbers of primitive people from their fellows. While the rest of the world struggled with wars and with conquering other people, the Atlanteans, as they called themselves, focused all their efforts towards harmonious endeavours. True, being human there were always plenty of Atlanteans interested in the more destructive ways of living. But, being largely outnumbered, and with a sophisticated yet workable system of law and order in place, the troublemakers were invariably banished into the mountains. A handful of such people would eventually reach the far side of the mountains, where their stories of the hidden kingdom would sustain them for the rest of their lives. As these travellers embellished their tales-in-the-tavern in the shade of the mountains, the country of Atlantis became the stuff of legend.

By the year 1959 BC the citizens of Atlantis were enjoying prosperity, enlightenment and plenty to eat and drink. The population swelled, as the average life expectancy was a hundred years. And while the country forgot that there was anything beyond the mountains, they became knowledgeable about every single thing within. The libraries in their many splendid cities bore testimony to their intense thirst for more and more practical knowledge; there were universities everywhere, full to the brim with brilliant minds, all clamouring for - and receiving - the opportunity to test their ground-breaking theories.

In the suburban sprawl of Altabar, nestled close to the western edge of the country, lived a man called John. Living in a small house with his wife Sarah, John was a caretaker at his local university. The pay was enough to keep himself and his wife comfortable, and he enjoyed his work. Indeed, he would often work until late into the night, causing Sarah to be suspicious that her husband was secretly seeing another woman. Which he was, usually. While John was a handsome young man with plenty of offers from pretty young student girls, Sarah was stunningly attractive herself and was constantly warding off advances from would-be suitors.

However, the night when Sarah decided to catch John *in flagrante* was the night he was becoming seriously absorbed in a book he had found earlier that same day. The book was about chemistry – though he had come upon a chapter that seemed more the stuff of alchemy – and he was in his office, alone, his mind reeling with the concepts it had revealed to him, when his wife walked in.

When she touched his shoulder and spoke his name, John's face was a picture of complete amazement, though not at her surprise appearance. He put down the book and took her hands. Sarah looked into his eyes, mystified.

"What?"

"Have you ever thought of being able to live forever, Sarah?" His young, pretty wife was scared that her husband was just losing his mind and not having an affair, after all. Unable to form a response, Sarah watched him carefully as he let go of her hands and picked the thick book up from the table.

"It's all in here, Sarah! It's – everything! Here! And *I* know how to do it!" His wife sat down, unable to do anything but listen to him describe how wonderful it would be – never growing old, never dying – his hawk-like eyes ablaze and his handsome features animated.

When, eleven years later, John returned from another late night at the university, he was drunk. John didn't normally drink much and Sarah assumed that he had been celebrating a friend's birthday or something. He had never spoken again about the book, or his plans for immortality to his wife, since the night she had found him in his office. Indeed, Sarah had forgotten all about that night, having spent the past ten years raising their two children, Aquileno and Lilith. And while John had been either working on some strange elixir or other in a long series of passionate encounters with any number of girl students, Sarah had managed to become pregnant by a rugged young gardener during one of her many clandestine liaisons with him.

When Lilith had been born into the world it had been obvious that John was not the father, but, having both sworn to stay with one another for the rest of their natural lives, a divorce, in Atlantis, was unheard of. John and Sarah remained together, growing old and still pursuing barely-concealed affairs, while their offspring both reached ten years old and, physically, remained ten years old, though the boy, Aquileno, was two years older than his sister.

The night when John had staggered home drunk, he had been celebrating - though it had been no one's birthday. Earlier that evening, after a secret meeting with another smitten girl student at the university, John had let himself into the laboratory and set up a curious assemblage of apparatus, working closely to the instructions in the book. One of the 'ingredients' was a small piece of rock that glowed unhealthily in the shadow of a large pot of bubbling purple goo. He tried not to touch it or even to stay too close to it, but he knew it was responsible for the lethargy-inducing headache that slowed his movements and dulled his senses.

He tended the large pot and the various other vats and cauldrons assembled around him, poring over every word in the book and making sure he followed every instruction to the letter. This kind of thing was far too dangerous to undertake more than once in any one person's lifetime - but then if it was performed properly, another attempt would not be necessary. This drove John throughout the night, his movements increasingly hampered by the close proximity of the ghastly vapours and fumes, but nevertheless he forged on.

Just when he was beginning to wonder if he'd be physically able to go the distance, he found himself turning the page over and seeing the last paragraph of the chapter. Forcing his brain to decipher the remaining instructions, John looked into the small crucible and realized that he had succeeded. The residue was a fine pile of dust in a rich and sumptuous shade of green that John had never seen before.

Taking twenty minutes to gather himself, John painstakingly poured the dust into a small pot, which he sealed carefully and put into his bag. After a few celebratory ales on the way home, he came home to find Sarah in bed with another gardener. In the ensuing physical set-to with the wife's latest lover, John's bag was dashed against the kitchen wall and the elixir allowed to trickle, unnoticed, into an almost-empty jar of bran on the counter. John evicted the naked gardener, but it had taken him every ounce of his remaining energy to do so. Too tired even to berate his wife, John collapsed onto the bed and fell into a deep sleep, too far gone even to shrug off her arms as she cuddled up to him.

The next day was a public holiday in Atlantis, so Sarah left John to lie in and went to get their children's breakfast. When she emptied out the jar of bran into the children's breakfast bowls she didn't notice the green powder. She added the milk and passed the bowls to the waiting youngsters. While Aquileno and Lilith ate the bran, Sarah went to the large pantry outside and refilled the jar. Finding John's bag on the floor behind a basket, Sarah recalled the previous night's scuffle, when her drunken husband had ejected her new lover. She picked up the book from within the bag and read its title:

KEMESTREUS MOTARIKON

Distracted by her children's appeal for more milk, Sarah replaced the book in the bag and took the jug over to the table. As she was clearing up a few missed broken pots from last night's fracas, she heard her husband calling out to her.

Making sure the children were content, she went out to the bedroom. John, she noticed, appeared to be ill and was babbling at her urgently – though somewhat incoherently – from their bed. She sat on the edge and held his arms.

"What is it, John?" She continued to hold him, even though his skin was cold and clammy. He was pointing and trying desperately to tell her something. "My bag. Bring me my bag."

She was back with it directly, though John was obviously still unhappy about something. Something was missing from the bag.

Sarah cast her mind back to the previous evening, when John had staggered through the door. But what had he lost that could be so important?

"I wanted to give it to the kids" muttered John. He thrashed weakly in his tortured state for a few minutes, then collapsed into a coma that lasted three days.

"Can we go out to play now, Mummy? We've finished our breakfast!" Aquileno and Lilith were standing in the bedroom doorway, side by side. Sarah ushered them out of the room and instructed Aquileno to put away his football and run to fetch the doctor. She returned to her husband and wiped his face with a clean cloth. She kissed his forehead. She would always love him, despite all their failings.

When John eventually recovered from the fever, he appeared to have forgotten all about the book and the missing whatever-it-was from his bag – even when their two children stopped ageing. It did not, however, escape the notice of the schoolteachers, nor subsequently, the local authorities, who launched a thorough enquiry into the whole business. Eventually, it was decided to banish the two children into the mountains, where they walked and climbed their way into the outside world, leaving their parents to live on without them. John continued working at the university and fooling around with a never-ending supply of besotted young girl students, while Sarah, having run out of gardeners, had taken a shine to the local baker – though there were to be no more 'buns' in her oven.

Some years later, when John and Sarah had grown old and died, and when Aquileno and his half-sister Lilith had travelled half-way around the world, the planet Venus, having received an even larger asteroid strike, had been deflected out of its orbit and collided with the Earth. Its touching point had been the hidden country of Atlantis, which, along with many of its vast mountain ranges, had been crushed and almost its entire population killed. Ironically, many of the sages had predicted the event shortly before it occurred, though nothing could be done to avert the catastrophe. A few who survived the devastating glance with the planet were unable to avoid certain death in the deluge which followed.

Within a few years Atlantis had been transformed into

a huge, inland sea and its former glories had become the stuff of legend and myth. Venus, spinning the wrong way and orbiting back in the direction it had come from, was never quite the same again either. There may be a man on the moon, but on Venus there is a small imprint of Atlantis, if you know where to look.

Chapter 20

1750 BC found the two immortal children amid a throng of merchants and luggage-laden travellers at the far-flung end of the European continent, as it would come to be known in later years, having stowed away in the hold of a departing vessel full of casks of fine wines from southern Italy. Already over two hundred years old, Aquileno and Lilith had become wise to the world and had developed a knack of not being noticed – of moving unseen – and this had, once again, enabled them to gain a passage to this other part of the planet. During the tumult of the unloading of the heavy cargo, Aquileno and his half-sister made good their disembarkation, both seeming to stroll merrily down one of the many planks to slip invisibly into the crowd on the quay, near a place known as the City of Lions.

As they walked hand-in-hand along the busy harbour street, Lilith remembered something and took a coin from the pocket of her faded brown smock. "Look what I found on the floor back there in the ship, Aquileno!" she said.

They stopped outside a craft workshop and he took the proffered coin from Lilith's tiny, delicate fingers, holding it up to the light and training his hawk-like eyes on the imprint, taking in the heavy gold content and noting the horns on the reverse.

"By all the gods, Lilith - this *is* a rare good find! Shall we buy something? Food?" They both shrugged at this suggestion as it seemed that while they both could eat, drink and digest as normal, there often seemed little point, as they had both survived years without normal sustenance during these early wanderings. Lilith looked beyond Aquileno at the various coloured and patterned bags and sacks hanging in the doorway of the craft workshop and something deep within her took a flying leap.

Her eyes, which now contained the same strange hawk-like quality as her half-brother's, were staring through the narrow opening of the small wooden dwelling and watched an emaciated woman trying to feed thin, cheap gruel to a tiny infant among the shadows within. Lilith and Aquileno walked up to the door just as a boy, a wiry eight-year-old, got up from inside the doorway, where he greeted them with a smile - which faded to a look of dejection when he saw that the would-be customers were only children like himself.

"Hello" said Aquileno, pretending not to notice the boy's disappointment. "What's that?" he added, indicating a dark, round thing in the corner. The effect on the boy was immediate.

"It's mine! You can't have that! It cost me a whole shilling!" The boy had picked up the object and was clutching it to his chest protectively, but Aquileno was intrigued.

"If that's a football then it's the first one I've seen in – " Here he had to pause slightly before finishing with "quite a long time! Can you play?"

At this, the boy's attitude changed remarkably. He turned to look back at the frail young woman feeding her other child. "Mama, can I go out and play for a little while, please?"

The woman's reply was inaudible but seemed to be in the affirmative. The young boy led Aquileno and Lilith down a little street that wound sinuously around the scattered shops, workshops and hovels until they reached a flat patch of green at the edge of the village. The boy signalled for his strange new companions to wait at the near end of the green and marched some forty yards away from them. Then he placed the ball carefully on the ground and began a long run-up at it. Aquileno winced as the boy punted it with the front of his toes and promptly fell on the floor, clutching his foot.

His face a mask of pain and wounded pride, the boy looked up at the two older children. "Why does it *hurt* so much when I kick the ball? It never seemed to bother my Papa when he used to still play."

Both Aquileno and Lilith passed on their skills to the boy (in Atlantis, the game had always been played with teams of men and women – that was half the fun!) who quickly learned several different ways of kicking it, swerving and dipping it and also taught him all the proper rules of the sport.

Afternoon was drawing into evening when they returned to the workshop. The boy's mother was, despite her tender years, hobbling around the dingy interior like an old woman, preparing food – such as there was – for her children's evening meal. The infant was lying on a thin cloth on the floor and crying, albeit weakly. The immortals glanced at each other and nodded.

"We would like to buy something." Lilith tried to smile at the woman's curious glance, though her heart was breaking with pity. "Please?" Here her voice cracked and it was all she was able to do to stop herself from crying. The woman waved an arm towards the collection of bags in the doorway and raised an eyebrow. Aquileno selected a dull, plain brown sack from the bottom of a pile of the cheapest bags and held the coin out to the woman.

"Is this enough?" asked Aquileno. She took the coin and shuffled to the doorway with it, examining it in the failing evening light. Then she tried to give it back, shaking her head and smiling.

"With this you could buy our whole shop! I cannot give you enough change from this. I am sorry." She took Aquileno's hand with both hers and forced the coin back into his grasp. Lilith quickly took the coin from his hand and pressed it back into the hand of the thin woman.

"We don't want any change, thank you" she said. "But please go and buy yourself and your children some proper food." Aquileno and Lilith walked towards the door, though it was the boy who stopped them. His mother, dumbfounded by this sudden change of fortune, was still comforting her smaller child.

"Take this, please" said the boy. "With the money you've given us I'll be able to buy a new one!"

Aquileno took the ball from the boy and thanked him. "Now I have something to carry around in my new bag!" he said.

The woman came to the doorway and insisted that they both stay for a meal and some shelter for the night. The boy was despatched to the shop for provisions, and the woman, her infant in her reanimated arms, motioned to them to make themselves comfortable in the small hut. As she busied herself preparing for the arrival of the food, the woman introduced herself.

"I am Arianna and my son is Samuel, named after his father. This" she said, smiling down into the face of her six-month old child, "is Lilith. My husband was a fisherman. Very big, good at his job and clever with his hands, too. It was he who made the bags when he wasn't at sea." Here her mood darkened. "But one day last year he never came back. There was a big storm and neither his boat nor the rest of his crew were ever seen again." There was an awkward silence for a while, then she continued.

"Since then I have had to bring up our children on what we can get from selling the bags. It has been hard."

It was at that moment that Samuel reappeared with two large bags crammed with fresh meat, fruit, vegetables and bread. As Arianna put the meat and vegetables into the pot and began cooking the meal, baby Lilith, her tiny stomach void of proper nutrition, began to cry. Samuel went straight to his baby sister and picked her up, cradling her in his lean arms and rocking her gently, cooing all the while, though it seemed to have little effect on her pitiful sobbing. The older Lilith began to sing softly and though her voice was quiet, the baby responded instantly, looking curiously at her brother's face above her. Lilith continued her song until the meal was brought in on simple wooden plates and bowls. As soon as she stopped, the baby began crying again, but now there was a wholesome broth to quieten the storm and the mood was good.

It was late when the meal was finished and Arianna was preparing to give Aquileno and Lilith her own bed to sleep in for the night. Samuel and his baby sister were already fast asleep and enjoying good dreams. Aquileno and Lilith, both experiencing odd physical sensations that neither had an explanation for, had both protested that the woman should sleep in her own bed, but she was having none of it. Her visitors exchanged a puzzled glance as they arose to the sound of the distant, hauntingly familiar melody of Lilith's earlier lullaby, seeming to lure them to the door.

Turning from her exertions, Arianna had thought of another reason why the two strangers should have her bed. But the reason was suddenly forgotten as she realised that they had gone before she'd even asked them their names. She glanced at the peaceful countenances of her two sleeping children and then dashed outside. Looking for them down the road in the direction of the quayside, she then thought to look the other way and froze. After a moment of stunned shock, she ran back into the hut and shook Samuel roughly awake.

"Quickly, my darling! Come and see!"

Still bleary after having been wrenched from a wonderful dream, Samuel's eyes were now two wide saucers. Neither he nor his mother were able to talk as they watched the distant figures of Aquileno and Lilith walking away, some two hundred yards up the track towards the east. The strange children seemed to have glowing white wings on their backs. The strain of Lilith's earlier song drifted back to them on the still night air and filled mother and son with unimaginable wonder.

The following morning, a familiar vessel moored at the quay. Almost the whole population of the village came to see this almost-forgotten local character skip from the prow of his boat as his crew tied it to the moorings. Samuel shook hands and made perfunctory explanations for his long absence, but his gaze was still casting about for any sign of his wife and children. Leaving his crew to unload the packed hold of fish, the big, bearded man strode away.

When he walked into the hut, his children were still asleep, though his wife was stirring in her bed. He knelt beside her and gasped involuntarily at how thin she had become.

"Arianna! It's me, Samuel! I've come home!" The woman's eyes were wide with wonder. She wept and threw her arms around him, hugging him and repeatedly looking hard into his face to make sure that this wasn't just some awful trick. Her reply, however, threw him completely.

"Oh Samuel! We had two angels here last night! I was wondering how much longer we'd be able to survive and two *angels* came and saved us! And my wonderful husband is home!" She kissed his thickly-bearded face until it had dissolved into a long series of smiles. When Samuel turned to see his son, Arianna danced through the door in a state of high elation and sang as she prepared a welcoming meal outside.

"Samuel, what's this your mother is talking about? Angels?" The man's questioning was cut short by his son's arms being suddenly wrapped tightly around his neck.

"Papa! You're back! Where have you been?"

Samuel explained how his boat had been caught up in a terrible storm that had dragged them right across the ocean to a strange land where the natives painted themselves and hunted big cattle with bows and arrows. The tale took a long time to relate and soon they were all seated and enjoying more of the delicious broth that Arianna had made the night before.

"So what's all this about angels then, young Samuel?" His son's grin stretched from ear to ear and he nodded.

"Yes Papa. We were visited by *two* angels last night. But we didn't know that's what they were when they first came here."

"And what did they do, these angels?" Samuel glanced at his mother before replying.

"They bought a bag." The tall, bearded man put down his bowl and leaned back.

"What type of bag – one of the pretty ones?" His son shook his head.

"No, Papa. They chose a plain brown one – but they paid with a whole ox!"

At this, his father was taken aback. He looked to his wife for confirmation and noted her seraphic smile and her nod. She produced a leather pouch and emptied out a pile of coins.

"This is the change that Samuel brought back after buying all the food that we now have!"

Samuel could see that there was still quite a fortune there. "And what did you give to these angels in return for all this wealth, Arianna?" At this the woman looked guilty and looked down at the floor.

"Food, drink, shelter for the night – though they did not stay long after the meal." Samuel was mystified and was about to start getting angry when his son cut in.

"I gave them my ball, Papa. They taught me how to play it properly and – I had nothing else to give them, Papa." Samuel sat back and regarded his wife and son gravely.

"What sort of men were these angels, then?"

"They looked like they were children, Papa. A boy and a girl. They were both very good at football. You should see what I can – " But he broke off, remembering that he had given away his ball and would not be able to demonstrate his newly-learned skills to his father. Samuel looked from his son to Arianna and, his eyes smouldering beneath his thick, bushy brows, spoke:

"Arianna. You are looking particularly beautiful today.

What do you say that we go up to the town and buy you some new clothes? And while we're at it, we'd better buy young Samuel here a new football!"

Chapter 21

As they set off out of the village the starlight from the cloudless night sky seemed to lend an extra quality to the air, somehow. Aquileno was glad they'd given the money to the poor family, but he couldn't bear the thought of imposing any more hardship on the kind Arianna by forcing her to sleep a night on the floor, though it was clear that the woman was more than happy to do so. Lilith was experiencing the same internal anguish as they slipped through the darkness. Strains of the same melody would return occasionally, and the physical feelings within them began to intensify until they could no longer ignore them.

When they turned to each other to speak, both were startled by the sight of the other, pointing wordlessly.

"What are those things on your back, Lilith?" asked Aquileno, His half-sister craned her neck around and saw that she, too, had what appeared to be glowing white wings waving majestically behind her.

"Let me see yours and I'll tell you." Aquileno was shocked to see that the same thing was happening to him. For a few moments in the dark, the waves lapping against the ancient shores of southern Lyonesse within earshot, the two immortals stood next to one another while each stroked the silky-smooth feathers of the other's ghostly wings, Aquileno looking towards the sea, Lilith facing inland.

When they awoke the next morning, the rain was lashing against the entrance to the cave that had sheltered them for the night. Aquileno was the first to come to. He noticed the wolf with her litter of cubs cowering in the cave's deepest corner, staring at him apprehensively. Then Lilith opened her eyes, still cuddled up to her half-brother, and noticed that their wings had gone, along with the strange sensations they had both experienced the night before. "Our wings have gone" she said.

Aquileno put a finger to his lips and indicated the wolf family just yards behind him. Lilith raised herself on an elbow and peered at the creatures.

"Hey, our wings have gone!" said Aquileno, eventually noticing the fact for himself. Lilith gave him a look of slight exasperation and sat against the side of the cave, rubbing her back along the earthy wall, searching for any remaining evidence of the alarming transformation. Aquileno lifted the back of his smock, but Lilith could find nothing to suggest that they had ever had wings at all.

Waving cheerfully to the wolf and her cubs, they marched out into bright sunshine, the rain having been just a passing shower after all, and walked towards the rising sun.

"I'm so glad we helped that family, Aquileno" said Lilith. "I was so sad when I saw Arianna through the doorway. She looked so thin, and yet she must be very pretty, really." The path was taking them up to the brow of a steep hill and the sun was still in their faces.

"I feel the same way myself. Samuel will be a great football player. Maybe his father will return and buy him a new ball?"

Lilith gave him another look of exasperation, which also afforded her momentary respite from the glare of the sun. "Life isn't just a fairy tale, you know! And you know very well that his father went to the deep with his boat and all his crew a year ago in a big storm. You heard what Arianna said - *whoa!*" The sun had dipped behind a cloud as, cresting the hill, they almost stepped out into thin air.

Holding on to one another, Aquileno and Lilith looked down at where the track and practically all the soil beneath and around it had fallen away. Moving carefully, they skirted the crumbling chasm where the incoming tide was whipping the dirt away in its wake and carrying it out to sea. Eventually the land became firmer again, but they were more cautious as they walked on.

"I can't remember those wolves being in the cave when we found it last night, can you?" said Lilith. Aquileno thought back, but he couldn't recall them either. He remembered that the light from the wings had bathed the cave walls with amazing shadows. He could remember stroking Lilith's wings as they cuddled together for sleep. He didn't think he was ever likely to forget that.

They regained the track that continued a quarter of a mile further along. Further east they could see the outline of a tall, steep mound, while the northern and southern shores threatened to converge in some places, where the sea seemed anxious to create islands, consuming the land in gargantuan chunks. They met other travellers as they went; they were mostly families fleeing the ever-encroaching ocean from all along the peninsula, trying not to notice their dwellings, barns and livelihoods being drawn, inexorably, crumbling into the waves as they went. Aquileno fell in beside a 14-year-old boy who was clearly struggling under his burden of a large sack of food, falling behind the rest of his family, all of whom bore similar-sized bundles of belongings and provisions.

"Hello, want some help?" Aquileno's offer had caught the youth by surprise and he stumbled, managing to cushion his precious cargo with his body as he hit the ground. Aquileno helped him to his feet and picked up one end of the sack. The boy looked at him uncertainly for a moment, then grabbed the other end and began to run until he had almost caught up with the rest of his folk.

The family stopped to rest beneath a broad, solitary oak, the sun beating down on it. The tall mound in the distance appeared to be no nearer than when Aquileno had first seen it. He and Lilith sat a little way away while the husband gnawed furiously on an apple and the wife tried to feed and impose order on their brood. The pieces of bread and the cheese the woman offered them were warmly accepted, though not eaten. The boy Aquileno had helped with the heavy sack was sitting between them and his family, the sunlight filtering through the leafy canopy and creating an almost impressionist scene.

His father called over to him. "Drustan!" The rest of the conversation consisted of nods in the direction of Aquileno and Lilith and movements with his dark eyebrows.

The boy turned to Aquileno and smiled sheepishly.

"Thank you for helping me to carry the food. I am in your debt." Lilith looked from her half-brother to the boy and then to his father, who was managing to smile contentedly as his jaws tore into a mouthful of bread. Two of Drustan's younger brothers scampered over to Aquileno and Lilith, nonchalantly relieving each of their meal and tucking into the extra portions with great gusto.

"Where are you all going, tell me?" asked Aquileno. Drustan glanced back at his father, but his father was engaged in removing more bread from the loaf in the sack the boy had been carrying.

"We're hoping to reach Kernow by tomorrow. Our village got swallowed by the sea and Papa is hoping to get work as a blacksmith in one of the big towns further east. We've been walking for three days now." His voice trailed off as he realized how tired he felt. If the friendly boy with the strange eyes hadn't stepped in when he had, he wasn't sure if he'd have been able to have gone the distance.

Aquileno and Lilith stood up together and smiled.

"Well, good luck to you all. We'll be on our way now. Thank you for the food." Aquileno swung the sack over his shoulder and turned to walk back out into the fierce glare of the midday sun.

"What's in the bag? Tell me." This was from Drustan. Aquileno and Lilith stopped and regarded each other momentarily, then turned around. Aquileno held the sack open and kicked the bottom of it. When the ball rocketed skywards out of the sack with a muffled thud and a *whoosh*, the whole family were taken by surprise. What really impressed Drustan was the way the strange boy caught the ball on his left foot without even appearing to look at what he was doing. Transfixed, Drustan stared at the ball which, even now, still nestled on top of Aquileno's foot.

"It's a football" explained Lilith. "I thought you had them here."

Drustan's father laughter was deep and loud. "Aye, child, but your brother has much skill for a boy of such tender years. Teach my son to play, will you?"

Drustan's tired eyes lit up and ran out into the sun, his exhaustion forgotten. Aquileno and Lilith spent the next hour showing him all the things they had taught Samuel the previous day before finally bidding a proper and final farewell.

As the sun began to set behind them, they at last reached the tall, steep mound they had been aiming for all day. Lying on its lower slopes, they rested for a while, drinking in the glory of the setting sun and looking out for any sign of Drustan and his family. When the old, bearded man came up and sat between them on the slope, nothing was said for several minutes, until the sinking sun, partially concealed by the hulk of a distant hill, was suddenly unmasked when the hill descended with a distant rumble.

"That's another beacon hill gone" said the old man. "What will become of the Summer Wedding if we can't light all the fires?" The question had obviously been rhetorical, but Lilith was intrigued by his words, even though she did not have not much to go on. "What is the Summer Wedding you speak of?" she asked.

Barely able to conceal his contempt at the girl's ignorance, the old man seemed ready to depart in a huff.

"The wedding of the Sun and the Land, of course! When the Sun stops in the midsummer sky we light the hill beacons across the Land. The Gods will take a poor view if the ritual is not religiously enacted. Crops will fail. Plague, pestilence and death shall ensue!"

Lilith made her way down to a small copse at the edge of a larger wood and seemed to stroll aimlessly about. The old man regarded her suspiciously, then turned to Aquileno.

"Do you children know nothing at all of these matters? Have you been bred in complete savagery?"

Aquileno smiled pleasantly, despite the old man's obvious scorn, saying nothing as they watched Lilith climb back up towards them.

"Well?" Lilith resumed her former position and smiled.

"Nothing to worry about. But we'd best get to Kernow soon or we'll have nowhere to sit." The old man stared at her.

"And the Wedding?" This came from Aquileno, though Lilith's reply was addressed to the old man. "Carry on lighting the fires from the ends of the land. The Gods understand when the sea becomes hungry. The land from Kernow to the east and its people are all safe. The Wedding will go ahead, believe me!"

The old man looked at her with open curiosity, watching as she got to her feet in the deepening twilight.

Aquileno got up and joined his half-sister as she walked off around the hill into the dusk.

"But how can you children know of such things?" asked the old man. He had left his question too late and he sat alone for a while, contemplating the girl's words, astounded by the calm certainty in her voice.

From the opposite direction came a family of weary travellers, unaware that they were about to meet a sage. The father of the roving clan asked how much further it was to Kernow.

"Just another mile or so" replied the old man. "You'll reach Porthgwarra and there you'll be safe."

The blacksmith was taken aback. "How do you know we'll be safe, old man?"

Feeling a little light-headed with his newly-acquired knowledge, the old man smiled mystically through his beard and turned to walk in the direction the children had taken.

"The sea is hungry – the Gods know this and understand! Follow me or you'll have nowhere to sit!"

Barely twenty minutes later, as the family made camp outside the village of Porthgwarra, a huge roar bore testimony to the wise old man's prediction. The beacon hill had been swallowed in one huge mouthful by the sea.

Chapter 22

Roy Marston's face was growing ever more flushed as he struggled to keep the ailing Austin A40 moving forward. He had removed his jacket and his shirt clung to his sweaty arms, making his movements more difficult as the sleeves twisted themselves into tourniquets. His wife Mabel suffered his verbal pleadings with the spluttering engine and tried to take an interest in the surroundings, unaware of the queue of vehicles stretched for miles behind them. They had driven down to Weston-Super-Mare for the weekend from their cramped flat in Birmingham, a short break from Roy's factory job and an excuse to stay in a guest house near the sea.

The weather had been perfect, and Mabel had had the good sense to liberally apply suntan lotion to both Roy and their 12-year-old son Michael, who had spent five whole shillings on the pier during a wonderful blur of excitement during the Saturday afternoon. His father, not a wealthy man by any means, was reaching into his pocket to continue the spree when his wife gently took his hand and shook her head, smiling. Michael would often think back to that weekend for several reasons; it was the most fun the family had ever had together; his father had treated him to a brand-new football from a sports shop in the town; *four* goes on the donkey rides and a vast, smooth sandy beach to try his new football out on, to boot! They ate ice cream and candyfloss; took a few long strolls up and down the promenade; had Sunday dinner at a café with a view of the sea, and built sandcastles. Michael's recollections were legion and detailed with smells of sea air and chip-shop fish.

Clutching his well-read and weatherbeaten *Beano Summer Special* and his new football, Michael sat on the back seat, willing the car to keep going. His father had a terrible temper at times, and the ailing motor car was, Michael feared, going to ring the bell at the top of his dad's blood pressure barometer. From his position behind the driver's seat, he could see that his father's left sleeve was torn from constant wrestling with the gear shift.

As the young boy began to fret about what his father might do if they broke down, he noticed a group of children playing football on a park not far from the road. They were very good. In fact, they were so good that Michael forgot to worry about his father, and moved over to the other end of the back seat for a better look. He watched the game carefully as the car began to seriously misfire and slow down, then bumped his forehead on the window as his father, finally admitting defeat, steered the car onto the pavement.

Roy looked at his wife, his face contorted by shame and misery as the vapour started hissing out from under the bonnet.

"Don't worry, love. There's sure to be a garage around can get us going again." Mabel's voice was soft and assuring.

Roy looked beyond her and pointed. "Maybe those lads can help us find one." He got out of the car and managed to lift the bonnet without getting scalded by the big clouds of steam, then set off into the park.

"Mum, can I go and play with my football on the grass there for a while?" asked Michael. "I won't go far, I promise."

Mabel turned and smiled at her son. "You might as well, Michael, it's a lovely day and we *are* still on holiday, after all."

"Thanks, Mum!"

Michael got out of the car and started walking towards where the children, having stopped their game, were standing around his dad. One of them set off at a headlong sprint across the park as he drew nearer, then his father was thanking the youngsters for their help and offering around boiled sweets from a paper bag.

Roy was walking back towards the car when he met Michael, still clutching his new football, coming the other way. They stopped and regarded each other.

"And where are you off to, young man?" said Roy.

"Can I have a quick kick-around while we wait for the car to be fixed, dad, *please?*"

Roy looked down at his son and then back at where the group of youngsters stood patiently waiting to resume their game. He thought how easy it had been to get help and quickly relented. Maybe the perfect weekend wouldn't be spoiled now, right at the end of their fun-packed summer break. Maybe there was no reason to get upset. Maybe they would be back in Birmingham before dark after all. "All right son, but make sure you're ready when the car's going again" he said. "I've got work in the morning and I want to get home."

He ruffled his son's hair and strolled back towards his wife, the impending storm having come to nothing.

After perfunctory introductions, Michael was chosen to replace the boy who had run off to fetch his older brother from the nearby garage and as he ran around and vied for the ball, Michael wondered vaguely where he was.

The children all seemed to be amazingly gifted, almost superhumanly quick and adept. They were performing elegantly-executed volleys and long, swerving passes with frightening exactitude. Yet long before the mechanic arrived, Michael was playing to the same level of excellence as the others, even fooling many of them completely with skills he had never possessed before. Within twenty minutes he felt as though he had been playing football with these children all his life.

Many of them were openly taken aback by how quickly this stranger had fitted in so perfectly with their game. Several were struck by how familiar Michael appeared to be. Likewise, practically all the youngsters seemed familiar to Michael, too.

"Come on team, stop gawping at the boy. We've got a game to play!" The rough-looking boy who had spoken dribbled the ball around everyone - players from both sides - as he attempted to revive the match. Gradually Michael's scrutiny became less intense. He ran after the rough-looking boy who had spoken and decided to tackle him. Brimming with a new-found confidence, Michael darted up behind him and prepared to surprise him from the right. But a split second before his foot would have made contact, the boy casually tapped the ball to his left and turned around, keeping his back to him all the time.

Michael grinned and attempted to go to his right again,

but with the same result.

For the next five minutes everyone else sat down for a rest as Michael persevered. Whatever he tried, the boy, who seemed to be a few years younger than himself, always ended up with the ball still at his feet and with his back to him. He began to wonder what he was doing wrong, especially after feeling so elated earlier on.

When Michael eventually gave up he flopped down on the grass with the others. Only then did the boy turn and face him, his face split with a cheeky grin and his hawk-like eyes flashing impishly.

"I was wondering where you were. Seems you were just born in the wrong place this time. Still, it was nice to have the whole team together again for a while."

Michael frowned as he tried to digest what the boy had just said in such a casual, offhand manner, then leaped to his feet, as the game was suddenly in full flight again.

An hour later and his father was calling to him from the road. The game, a hell-for-leather flurry of outstanding football, was suddenly over, Roy's call having the same effect as a long whistle from the referee. Michael picked up his football, a lump in his throat and tears welling in his eyes, then turned and looked around at the sad faces. As he walked away, the boy he'd been unable to tackle earlier called out to him.

"See you next time!"

The car was fixed and the fee had been affordable. Roy's mood had also been improved by an impromptu cuddle with Mabel in the car while they waited for the mechanic to arrive, so Michael's tears went unnoticed as they drove away. He stared at them intensely as the figures became smaller in the distance, trying to etch the memory in his mind so he wouldn't forget, his mind performing cartwheels all the while.

"Where was that place back there, Dad?"

His father, smiling broadly and exchanging secret looks with his wife, was back in good humour again. He took a piece of paper from his shirt pocket and handed it back to his son.

"Should be written on there somewhere, near the top?"

Michael took the small receipt and read it. It seemed that the problem had been a 'jarred something-or-other' and the man had charged his father four shillings for the repair. At the top was the mechanic's name and address with a phone number, slightly smudged and stained with oil.

Charlie's Garage, Church Lane, Steepledon 0272 - 64510

Chapter 13

26TH MARCH, 1205 AD

Aquileno's half-sister had spent hundreds of years wandering the face of the planet with him, learning all the skills of survival by watching the way he gradually developed a way of moving without being seen. Realising that the natural ageing process no longer applied to them, the strange-looking duo explored the world several times over. They witnessed events of global impact, from such disparate parts of the world, over a thousand years before Christ, that all records of them were lost and only fragments survived in parts of early chivalric romances - borrowed and pasted in by an unknown cleric from the depths of the aptly-named Dark Ages to pad out his own tale. They had endured hundreds of years of living in the wild, eating only occasionally, and it seemed that, as they were immortal, eating food was no longer necessary, though they both still enjoyed something now and again to nibble on. Until the end of the eighth century BC, they had stayed together throughout.

Aquileno had seen fit to change his name from time to time. When he had made his remarkable appearance at Tarquinii the people had named him Tages, and Aquileno went along with it. While he set himself the task of writing the Acherontian Books for these people, Lilith got a little bored and went for a wander on her own - not too far away, but never seeming to be able to meet up with him again. What drove both immortals on was the hope of becoming reunited, though their travels through the ensuing millennium covered millions of miles and, eventually, their memories of each other became buried under growing drifts of new ones.

But Lilith's memories of her half-brother refused to lie smothered. And when she heard the familiar sounds of a football match in the forest that day, she was excited, hoping against hope that she would be seeing her half-brother again.

When she stepped out of the cover of the trees and they saw each other, Lilith began to sing, wondering why it took him so long to reach her. Once she could see that he was on his way to her, she retreated back into the trees. Without even stopping to wonder at the thing's existence, she sat on a giant pink mushroom which she had somehow not noticed before, tearing off chunks and eating them. It didn't seem to taste of anything in particular, but it did help to clear her head a little.

She was disappointed that her half-blood relative was unable to properly remember her, though the mushroom he ate had obviously been having some effect before he suddenly vanished in front of her eyes. Feeling terribly cheated at the brevity of their meeting, she had wept for days on the mushroom before getting up and walking towards the setting sun, eventually falling asleep in a wood over a hundred miles away.

When she awoke she was aware that a lot of time had passed. While she thought about this, she stared at a tree nearby which, for no apparent reason, seemed familiar to her. She recognized the tree as being a yew and, without really understanding why, she never strayed far from it. She even made it her purpose to guard it and make sure that no harm ever came to it; incidentally, without her knowledge, she was spotted occasionally in the wood by children, and inadvertently became a 'wood fairy'. People would travel from far and wide for the wonderful good fortune that always accompanied a rare sighting of her.

Eventually the need to utilise the yew tree's wood for the manufacture of longbows disappeared. Over the years Lilith watched the tree and observed its gradual growth.

She noticed a hole in the trunk a little above her head open out and grow wider as the seasons came and went and generations of people were born, lived their lives and died. Once she fancied that she heard her name called from nearby, but there had been no one in sight. Something told her that the voice had come from the tree itself.

Then, one day, she went to sleep again and dreamed that she was inside the yew tree – not in any danger, but completely contained within its trunk, lulled by strains of marvellous music and suspended in an overwhelming feeling of warmth and security.

Chapter 14

Mark Lane had come to the city to get himself a job and somewhere to live and to attempt to straighten himself out after decades of alcohol and drug abuse. Ever since he had lost the rest of his family in a house fire, Mark had been going steadily downhill. Fighting the guilt of not having perished with his family, he lost his job as a theatre electrician in the Midlands, got thrown out of his flat when he stopped paying the rent and found himself wandering south west.

As he faced another long night with nowhere to sleep, Mark rummaged in the shadows among the litter, looking for anything that would give him some hope - something to cling to, something he could turn into some sort of a makeshift ladder which he could use to climb out of the mire his life had become. He stooped to turn over a pile of newspapers and his back creaked. Having found nothing of any use there, he straightened up his back and winced, his eyes taking in the strange, inverted step-like nature of the wall that sloped out above him.

As he walked back out and looked up at the broad, concrete sweep of the stadium's outer edge, something deep within him moved.

"Ah! Steepledon Rovers' old ground! Of course!" Thousands of memories stirred within him - mostly of watching Nottingham Forest with his younger brother, Will, who had perished in the fire along with his mother, father and sister when he was much younger. He remembered the games in the park from his youth. He had always loved football more than almost anything else and, even in his state of vagrancy, still knew that the club had, thanks to their current run of success, treated itself to a brand new stadium a few miles away in the countryside. The old ground was awaiting redevelopment into a new housing estate, but here the place still was, empty and inviting.

After a further hour shifting piles of rubbish, Mark found a door which would open just enough for him to squeeze through. When the rubbish he had cleared to get in fell back against the door and slammed it shut, he found himself in a musty and frightening atmosphere, compounded by complete darkness. Finding the stairs by falling onto them, Mark ascended them on his hands and knees, praying for a window to shed some light on where he was.

After continuing to climb this way for thirty minutes, he bumped his head on a wall and realised he'd reached the top. Groping around him in the darkness, he found the edge of a doorframe and moving slowly, located a handle. He turned the handle and pulled. Nothing. What he'd been expecting, really. There was a terrible pain in his chest and he was incredibly weary, though he didn't want to sleep on this cold, dark landing. He turned it again, pushed, and the door swung open.

The room's large interior had been cleared of any furniture there might once have been, but Mark's electrician's brain sparked to life when he saw that the 'Hermit' was still here. Walking over to the dust-smothered mass of antiquated machinery bathed in the dim glow from a large, picture window, Mark wiped it down with his sleeve and crouched down in front of the console, grinning. His rational mind was waiting, smugly expecting to pipe up with an 'I told you so' when he discovered that there would be nothing to power the thing with after all.

Astonishingly, the lights on the panel all began to flash into life.

Mark's rational mind stayed quiet. He was mystified, but

he had always dearly wanted to own a little HRMT set and now that they were being phased out, he had thought that he was going to miss his chance.

A large screen flickered into life and offered him a list of football matches to watch. Running over to the long picture window he was delighted to see that the holographic equipment was going through its warm-up; three-dimensional images were advertising big, lurid-looking hot dogs and the sound system was about to launch into a fanfare that would, if Mark wasn't fast enough, wake up the whole city and draw unwanted attention to himself before he'd had time to at least watch a few classic cup-ties.

Darting back to the console, he called up the audio section and dropped it to a whisper, then settled back to watch a few of the really good games he'd missed from the previous three years, silently wishing, all the time, that the rest of his family could be here to see it all, too.

After a while he began scrolling through all the games from down the decades. Mark was fifty-four years old and had been born in 2302, the year the HRMT had come into being. He felt as if he was scrolling back through his life as the year indicator next to the recorded matches drew closer to the year he had been born. The pain in his chest had gone and he no longer felt tired.

He glanced away as he caught sight of a movement in the room, putting it down to his imagination when his check revealed nothing. Returning his attention to the screen, it seemed he had selected another football match to watch, though he had not done so consciously. He looked at the information display quizzically as it took on a strange, pale-green tinge and flashed '1904' in the year column. The adjacent columns, where the teams and their player's names should have been, was obscured by the green glow.

Mark got up and walked over to the window. When he first looked down, he thought a group of kids had followed him in, but then he realised that the kids were holograms and were playing a football match. As he watched he realised that the children were tremendously skilled. He began enjoying the game more than any he'd ever watched before.

An hour or so later Mark went back to scrutinize the screen again. The children he'd been watching seemed slightly different, and he was determined to find out who they were. The green glare had faded slightly and he was now able to read some of the names:

"Joseph Green, Philip Donaldson, Jimmy York, William Browning, Robert Carlton... what?" He stopped as he saw the year indicator show 1962, and ran back to the window. They seemed to be the same children, wearing slightly different clothes, though the action was played at a wildly fast tempo.

Ten minutes later they had all changed again, all bar one, who appeared to be exactly the same person throughout. Mark thought he had seen the boy before somewhere. Many of the children, he noticed, looked very familiar, but none more so than the central defender with the strange eyes.

He went back to the console again and checked the display. The year was now 1935 and the teams (six-a-side) read: 'R. Wright, J. Foxton, J. Foxton. W. Green, D. Brown, P. Davidson, T. Jones, J. York, R. Organs, H. Gorman, R. Smith, T. Pebworth'. Mark went back to the window and looked down, amazed at the stamina and skill of the children way below on the pitch. He decided that he'd go down and take a closer look from the stand.

Finding a door at the far end of the long room, Mark opened it and gingerly poked his head around the corner. He didn't want to get lost and possibly lock himself out of the stadium, but he dearly wanted to get a closer look at the players on the pitch, especially the boy who he thought he'd seen before somewhere.

He sighed and closed the door, realising that he'd need a torch. Turning to walk back to the window, Mark's foot caught something metallic and sent it skittering across the floor. Reaching down into the gloom, his fingers closed on the handle of a torch and switched it on accidentally in the same movement.

"Yow!" he exclaimed. "Just the thing!"

Armed with a source of illumination, Mark strode back to the door and skipped confidently down the steps, finding a door to the stand far below. Emerging into the empty ground, Mark walked down to the edge of the pitch at the halfway line, his eyes glued to the holographically-reproduced football match as the children raced through the air above the turf. He sat down and watched as a corner kick was being taken, transfixed as the ball rebounded around the crowd of players in the goalmouth. Mark hadn't seen a goal go in yet, though the deadlock was surely going to be broken at any moment.

The defending goalkeeper was trapped under a pile of defenders and attackers and countless shots were rebounding off the crossbar, being headed off the line and cannoning off the post. Eventually, it bobbled over the touchline for a goal kick, but the children were all rolling around on the ground, laughing hysterically. It had seemed very comical to watch the melée, and Mark smiled to see that the children had also enjoyed it.

As the goalkeeper ran up to take the kick, the HRMT apparatus appeared to malfunction. Mark blinked as the players, all now wearing different clothes, ran upfield to follow the ball. One of the children caught the ball and lofted it back to the goalkeeper with a long kick. Mark frowned. He couldn't see why the goal kick had to be retaken.

The goalkeeper now appeared to be a lad in his mid-teens. Mark watched him take a fast run before punting the ball ferociously upfield. The other players were becoming a little out of focus as the ball whistled through a crowd of them, still rising as it approached the opposition's penalty area. Mark thought he caught a glimpse of something black in the air which exploded when the ball collided with it, directly above the goalkeeper. When the ball ricocheted downwards, hit the back of the goalie's head and bounced up and onto the crossbar, Mark was amazed, but when the ball came back out to bounce behind the goalie and spin back to dislodge the dead bird now on his head and *then* go into the goal, he laughed so loud and so long that his jaw ached and he fell to weeping uncontrollably.

Finally, drained emotionally and physically, he managed to open his eyes. He cast his tear-streaked face to the sky and saw that dawn was approaching. The children were back playing again. The ball had fallen to a little red-haired girl of no more than six, who effortlessly trapped it beneath a foot while an identical little girl swept the ball out to the wing. The ball fell to two eight-year-old boys, who played such a rapid one-two passing technique that Mark could never actually see which one of them had possession at any one time as they surged down the right wing. The ball was crossed over to a boy who appeared to celebrate his subsequent goal by turning into a seagull and flying into the air, becoming more and more indistinct the higher he rose above the hologram-generators beneath the pitch.

Jolted from his reverie by the unmistakable feeling of a hand on his shoulder, Mark spun around, positive that he'd been having another dream in someone's doorway. He began mentally preparing himself to spend another grim day foraging and begging.

The little boy who had been playing in every one of the children's football games was now sitting a few seats away from him.

"Hello Mark, we're going to have to leave now" said the boy with the mysterious, hawk-like features. He pointed towards the back of the stand, where uniformed policemen were emerging from the exits. Mark got to his feet, rather unsteadily, and looked down at him.

"Jimmy? Is it really you? Why do you look the same way you did when I was a boy?" Seemingly nonchalant about the presence of the approaching policemen, Jimmy smiled and leaned back, revealing a girl behind him who seemed to be younger still.

"He's not Jimmy. He is Aquileno, and I am Lilith, his half-sister" chuckled the girl, who had eyes like her brother's. The two figures got to their feet, took a hand each and escorted him to the edge of the pitch, the policemen now only yards behind them. Filled with a great sensation of well-being, Mark still expected to be grabbed by one of the policemen at any time, but the moment never came. He noticed that the field was now full of holographically-reproduced children, all walking towards the players' tunnel, though by the time they reached the entrance to the tunnel there were only twelve, the others all seeming to merge into the remaining dozen.

As they walked onto the pitch, two long rows of spectral archers sprang from the turf, defending the halfway line and leaving a line of escape for the three figures to follow where the group of children had just gone. The policemen scattered as the luminous arrows rained down on them, not realising that they were harmless until Mark, Aquileno and Lilith had reached the tunnel.

It grew darker and darker as they walked until the sound of the shouting policemen was far behind them. Mark could hear the chatter and laughter of children in the gloom up ahead. He moved his fingers to make sure the children were still leading him. Reassured that he was not alone, he sighed.

"You know, that reminds me of something from a book I read when I was about eight, *The Angels of Mons*" he said. "Did you ever hear that legend?"

Aquileno and his half-sister laughed in the echoing darkness, either side of him.

"That wasn't a legend, Mark" said Aquileno. "That actually happened. And we're going to tell you all about it."

Mark, now feeling dreadfully weary again, brightened as he noticed a light approaching them from the far end of the tunnel. The unmistakable shapes of his brother, sister, father and mother were coming towards him, looking exactly as he remembered them – their arms wide and welcoming. He let go of the children's hands and shouted with joy as he embraced the rest of his family. Now he had them back, he told himself, he would never lose them again.

The police had searched the entire stadium from top to bottom and found no sign of the vagrant, the two strange children or any of the several hundred spectral archers. Crowds of officers still stood on the edge of the pitch, staring down the players' tunnel and wondering where they could all have gone. Some of the more impressionable officers agreed afterwards that the children escorting the vagrant had big angel's wings, though nothing of that showed up in any official report.

Later on that morning, one of the policemen found the body of the vagrant in a pile of rubbish behind the stand. His drug-and-alcohol ravaged face wore a seraphic smile, despite the squalor and filth all around him.

41374788R00113

Made in the USA
Lexington, KY
17 May 2015